Finding Ann

To Boots —

Corinda Pitts Marsh

Hope you enjoy the story —

Corinda

Copyright © 2017 Corinda Pitts Marsh

All rights reserved.

ISBN: 1540506487
ISBN-13:9781540506481

DEDICATION

This story is dedicated to Ann and to her sisters all over the world who have lived hidden lives of abuse. May they find strength, freedom, and happiness while being loved, appreciated, and respected in a world that understands.

We are cats: we can't be controlled and we choose our own pride.
I choose you.

CONTENTS

	Acknowledgments	i
1	The Diaries	1
2	JT Stanton	20
3	Senior Year	34
4	Carousels and Ferris Wheels	55
5	Mrs. Beckham	77
6	Where is Ann?	115
7	The Reunion	131
8	Hiding Ann	142
9	Escape	158
10	Finding Ann	173

ACKNOWLEDGMENTS

Cover art by Dennis Perrin. Perrin is a painter of light, transforming human emotion into art through the use of light in all its forms. His love of beauty shines clearly in his paintings. His style is reminiscent of paintings by John Singer Sargent and Henri Fantin-Latour. His style is best described as Painterly Realism. He is a renowned artist and teacher based in York, Maine. His work can be viewed at Dennisperrinfineart.com.

It does not follow that the meaning must be given from above;

that life and suffering must come neatly labeled;

that nothing is worthwhile if the world is not governed by a purpose.

Walter Kaufmann

1
THE DIARIES

The package landed on my desk with little fanfare. It was on the bottom of the stack simply because of its size. Most were neatly addressed envelopes; a few were in large manila envelopes with ornate scrawls across the front; then there was the package from Indian Pass. I had absolutely no idea where Indian Pass might be, and I couldn't image a writer sending this unwieldy bundle of material thinking I would actually read it. Our office has clearly stated requirements for submissions, and this one, if it was actually a submission at all, was most definitely not within the guidelines.

I slid my letter opener under the tab on the end of the package and held the opening wide enough to see four old books inside. I started to shove it off the end of my desk into the half empty trash can. Then I saw it.

I recognized the spine of one of the books. I had one just like it when I was a young girl. The volume had a faded blue backing, but what caught my eye was the bird, or at least what was left of the bird embossed into the old leather. I knew what it looked like when it was new. My father gave me one on my fourteenth birthday. I wrote in it faithfully every day until I left for college. I had not thought about it since.

The volume I recognized was on the bottom of the stack of four nearly identical diaries. They were all the same size but different colors. One had a red smear on the bottom of its nearly new spine. It was less worn than the others, but it was the blue one I wanted to see.

As I thought, it was the diary of a young girl. She, too, had received the diary for her birthday. She was fifteen when she began to record her steps on its faded pages.

It was Friday afternoon, the final day in an exhausting week, so I was not eager to tackle another manuscript before I left for the weekend. This diary, however, refused to loosen its stubborn grip on my psyche. I stuffed it into my briefcase and snapped it shut.

I stood up and hesitated remembering the day I started writing in my diary. I stared at my desk and the clutter I was leaving, wondering how I got so quickly from there to here. I glanced out the window and sighed. Cars were rushing past in a Friday afternoon frenzy. Finally I picked up my jacket and briefcase and walked out. Computer keyboards hummed in a meaningless drone as my colleagues sped toward Saturday and a day without words lunging at them.

Jennifer was so focused on her screen that she didn't realize I was standing beside her. "Jennifer," I whispered. "I'm leaving. Have a nice weekend."

Jennifer jumped and spun around in her chair. "Oh,

I'm sorry, Dr. Prentice. I didn't realize you were standing there. We have twenty-three new manuscripts to format, so I was trying to get one more done before I leave."

I laughed and replied, "No problem. My brain is fried, so I'm leaving a little early. I'm going to the coast for the weekend. I need salt air to blow the sludge out of my brain." I tapped Jennifer's desk and added, "Don't work too hard, kiddo. It will all be here Monday when we get back."

Jennifer smiled and said, "I'll remember that next week when you want to know why I'm not finished."

I waved to her over my shoulder as I walked out the door. The air was wet and steamy but the sky was blue to the east, so I got in my car and headed for the coast. Canaveral was only fifty miles from my office, but Friday afternoon traffic crept along at a snail's pace, so I didn't see the ocean until the horizon had begun to fade.

The ocean was a calm and mysterious Prussian blue with faint glimmers of reflected light eating the breakers. Three pelicans sailed past my balcony on heavy, wet ocean winds. From the fourteenth floor I could look straight out into the sky without interference from earthlings walking beneath me on the beach. I was alone in my quiet world. The reverie was rippled only by the roar of the surf and distant calypso music.

I poured myself a drink and clutched the remains of the tired blue bird. The constant onslaught of salt air accumulating in the track of the sliding glass door resisted, but I gave it an extra shove and walked into the twilight sky. I brushed off my chair and set my drink on the small glass table beside a pink conch shell then sat down with the blue bird on my lap. I ran my hand over the soft leather and felt the impression of the bird, worn as she was.

Suddenly I remembered Bobby Johnson and wondered what ever happened to him. Finally I took a deep breath and opened the diary, half expecting to see my own childish scrawl on the page. I didn't. It was Ann's diary.

The inscription on the first page was, *"To Ann, my sweet baby. May this book be filled with happy memories for you to hold dear for the rest of your life. Love, Daddy."*

Ann's handwriting was the neat and studied hand of a perfectionist. Even in this informal medium, every "i" was dotted and every "t" was crossed. Each paragraph was indented the width of a woman's finger. Inside the first page was a brittle, faded, pressed rose. The rose appeared to have been pink when it was young. I set it carefully aside and read the first page.

By midnight, Ann was my closest friend. I knew her. I felt her tears on my cheek. She had kept the smallest details in her diary, making me wonder if she had ever shared them with another human being. The book seemed to be her only confidante. Why had she trusted me with the blue bird? Why me and why now?

I couldn't imagine her sharing with a perfect stranger thoughts she had held only in her own beating heart for a lifetime. I had to know. I knew about volume one of her life, but I wanted more. I went to bed and woke with the sun the next morning. I dressed quickly and got into my car, driving toward Ann and away from the rising sun.

Traffic was sparse at that hour, so I reached my office before 8:00 am. I rode up the elevator tapping my keys impatiently against my side. I heard their jingle and the hum of the rising elevator amplified by my impatience. I hurriedly went inside and retrieved the package.

I dared not unsheathe any of the volumes until I reached my balcony once again. I was tempted to read while driving as my best friend in college had done, but I had not grown so brave or foolish with age.

I forced myself to take my time like savoring Christmas morning, but it wasn't easy.

By the time I got home, the sun had risen high enough for the balcony to be shaded. I settled into my chair once more. In the early afternoon I forced myself to put the third volume down and break for lunch, but I stared at the book the entire time. I wanted to find Ann and cuddle her in my arms to stop her shaking. I could feel her trembling even after I put the book down. I read stories every day as a part of my job, but today I was reading a life, not a story.

Ann's life appeared from the outside to be a fairytale, but the only similarity to a fairytale, was the big, bad wolf in her life. And even he was disguised and unrecognizable to all but the most astute of observers.

Before the sun came up Sunday morning, I had finished reading Ann's story. I was exhausted from the sheer terror of it, but at the same time I was energized beyond belief. I had to find Ann and talk to her in person. I had to see the woman who had lived this nightmare in silence. If I had anything to say about it, she would never be silent again, and I *would* have something to say about it.

I dialed Jennifer's extension and said, "Cancel my appointments for Monday and Tuesday and get me an appointment with Max on Wednesday. Tell him I have our next million seller. I'm going to Indian Pass. See you

Wednesday."

Ann had included her phone number with her diaries, so promptly at 8:00 am I called her.

She answered, "This is Ann."

"Ann, my name is Emily Prentice. I am the Wollstonecraft Books agent who received your package. I'd really prefer to speak to you in person and as soon as possible. Where exactly is Indian Pass?" I asked.

"Ms. Prentice, I'm so pleased to hear from you. And yes, I would love to meet with you. Indian Pass is about twenty miles west of Apalachicola. Where would you like to meet?" Ann asked politely.

"I would like to come to Indian Pass to see where you live. I vacationed in Apalachicola a few years ago, so I am familiar with the area. I feel as though I've known you all my life. I've read your diaries, and believe me, I am *not* afraid to come to your venue. Your ex may be ten feet tall and bullet proof, but he is not Emily Proof. May I come to your home today to speak with you?" I asked.

"Certainly, Ms. Prentice. I would be thrilled to talk to you. I live in a small cottage near the end of the Indian Pass Road. It's easy to find. Just turn at the Raw Bar and keep going until you see the boat landing at the end of the road. I'll meet you there. My friend owns the store at the landing. He keeps an eye on me, and he won't let anyone bother us," Ann said.

"Oh believe me, honey, no one is going to bother us, at least not for long they won't. I will leave Canaveral in the next hour and will be there before nightfall. I'll bring the diaries with me. I just have to ask, do you live in the cottage in the story, the one where you made love to JT?" I asked.

"Why yes, I do. I suppose you think that odd that I shared that detail with you," Ann said.

"Not at all. I think it is a beautiful story. May I ask if he is in your life now?" I asked.

"No, I haven't seen him since our 20th class reunion. I don't know where he is. I live here alone," Ann told me.

"I look forward to meeting you, Ann. Your story touched my heart. I think you have more sisters than you can imagine. We can discuss what to do with this story when I get there. Take care and stay safe. I will see you before the sun sets today," I told her. We hung up. I smiled and I'm sure Ann was standing there with her phone in her hand, stunned and maybe a little apprehensive. I didn't intend that, yet I'm sure it happened. Sometimes my enthusiasm gets the best of me.

I crossed the Apalachicola Bay bridge shortly before 4:00 pm. Seeing the quaint fishing village made me smile until I realized Beecher Beckham lived there. The smile froze and became revenge. I wanted to be the sword that impaled Beecher the Brute, and I would, one way or another.

A sign west of town told me Indian Pass was 12 miles. I veered onto the two-lane road and the landscape evolved. Gnarled pines twisted from repeated hurricanes grew along the roadside in dense thickets. Palmettos poked their blades through the thicket like green fingers. Two blue herons stalked the ditches. Their spindly legs looked unable to hold their bodies, but somehow they maintained a graceful stance as their eyes darted about. One spied a fish and jabbed his bill into the water like a lightning bolt. His head emerged with a fish flapping out either side of his bill.

I was driving along thinking of Ann when I saw a throng of cars parked all around the road ahead. Then I saw the sign. "The Raw Bar." I had heard of this place but had never seen it. It was not what I expected at all. People lolled about on an open porch waiting to get inside. It was a dump, but apparently it was true to its reputation: it has the best seafood in North Florida. Ann had said, "Turn at The Raw Bar."

A smaller two-lane paved road ran perpendicular to the infamous Raw Bar. I turned left and continued into Old Florida. The landscape looked like it came straight out of a Marjorie Kinnan Rawlings novel. I crossed a narrow bridge over a bayou mostly filled with reeds. Channels of lazy brackish water snaked through dark creases in the forest of reeds. The road veered east. I began to see more dunes of white sand, but even they had wise trees growing but gnarled by time and experience. Their shadows seemed dark and magical. A few cottages nestled into the groves, but I still felt alone in a natural but unnatural world.

I came over a small rise in the pavement and saw red water set ablaze by a sinking sun. Directly in front of me was the boat landing Ann had described. As I got closer, I was struck by the beauty but even more by the isolation. Three fishermen loitered around boats on trailers with salt water still dripping from their transoms, but other than that, I saw no one. The small camp store Ann had mentioned was open, but I saw no customers. Beer signs covered most of the windows. One had two large ads for Florida Lotto and five different ads for live bait. A rack of fishing poles leaned precariously against the side of the weathered old building. The building reminded me of a wooden lapstrake boat. My guess was that whoever built it might have been more accustomed to building boats than buildings. I suppose it is what Chip and Joanna Gaines call shiplap.

I parked beside the store and got out. I leaned back and stretched the miles out of my bones then started toward the water. Two of the fishermen watched me. When I walked past them they both spoke at the same time. One asked, "You lookin' for somebody, Ma'am?"

The second man mumbled something I couldn't understand.

I answered, "Yes, as a matter of fact, I am. I am meeting a friend. She said she would be here."

"Yes, Ma'am. I think that's probably Miss Ann. She's down yonder at the point. Just stay on that little path. I reckon she's walkin' the pelicans home to roost," said the man. He slung his cooler in the back of his truck and jerked the door open with a loud screech before he stopped and looked down the path. I wondered why he stood there so long. Finally he noticed I was watching and tipped the bill of his cap and nodded his head then got in his truck and drove away, his trailer and boat obediently following him across the bed of oyster shells and onto the gravel road. The outline of a rifle hanging behind his head in the cab of the truck was clearly visible. I assumed he knew how to use it and might not hesitate to do so.

The weather was pleasant but clouds were gathering over the island across from the ramp. A sign beside the ramp posted ads for tours of St. Vincent's Island, so I assumed that was the spit of land across from the ramp. It looked like a typical barrier island off Florida's coast, but it interrupted the clouds in just the right places. The scene would have made a nice painting, but it was so typical I might not have paid much attention if not for the clouds.

Sea oats atop the dunes on the island threatened to puncture the balloon clouds. Upper level winds were whipping the clouds along at a fast clip while the sun settled into the Gulf. Being accustomed to sunrise over the ocean, I was enthralled by the sunset on this side of Florida. For the span of a breath, I forgot why I was here. Then I saw Ann walking up the beach toward me. She waved to me and quickened her pace.

I walked toward her, watching her body language as she approached. Her steps were more lively than I expected. After reading her diary, I wanted to hug her and protect her, but seeing her took away my pity. She smiled softly as she came nearer. Her smile was genuine, no hint of trauma in it.

"You must be Ann," I called out when she was near enough to hear me.

"Yes, ma'am. That would be me, and I'm guessing you are Ms. Prentice," she replied.

"No, I'm Emily," I answered, extending my hand.

Instead of shaking my hand, Ann reached out to hug me. "You are in the real South now. We hug people we like," she said as she put her arms around me.

It would have been impossible not to respond to this warm, beautiful woman.

Ann linked her arm in mine and said, "Let's go home. I don't live very far from here, but you'll want to drive your car because you can't leave it parked here overnight. You are spending the night aren't you?"

"Yes, of course. We have a lot to talk about. Should we make arrangements for my lodgings before we go to your house? I suspect that rooms here might come at a premium," I said.

Ann laughed and said, "Oh, I wouldn't worry too much about that unless you are the picky city sort."

"Why no, I'm not especially particular, but I haven't seen any hotels since I left Apalachicola," I answered.

"No, there aren't any hotels here, just a few of us friendly locals who are a mind to take in a stranger now and then. If you don't mind keeping company with a lazy cat, you are most welcome to stay with me. I'd love the company, and I have already fluffed your pillow. I assumed you would stay with me," Ann said as if she had known me all her life.

I looked at her and shook my head. "You really are who I thought you would be. You just invited a complete stranger to spend the night in your home. I might be an ax murderer," I said.

"I'll take my chances," said Ann. We both laughed and the lines relaxed on both our faces.

We breathed the clean salt air as we walked to my car. Her world was all around me. We walked up to my car, and I stood for a long moment looking at her standing beside the car waiting for me to unlock the door. We were suspended in time. It was one of those moments you always remember but you don't know why.

Ann's face was pale. Her gray-streaked sandy brown hair was neatly tucked into a twist on the back of her head, but small wispy curls straggled loose in the wind and danced with her cheeks. She shook her head and let the wind blow the curls around. The feathery stragglers flew out of her line of sight. I knew she was assessing me as well.

When I became aware of our eye lock, I pressed the key fob to open the doors and said, "Step into my chariot, and we shall begin this adventure."

And begin we did. It was the start of a chapter I will forever remember.

Shortly after we pulled away from the boat landing, Ann directed me to turn onto a path lined with oyster shells. The shells crunched beneath my tires and small branches brushed the windshield twice. The lane twisted about so that I could not see the cabin until we were only twenty yards from its front porch.

Ann lived in a small Florida Cracker house with a rusted tin roof and a generous screened porch with rocking chairs. I thought Marjorie Kinnan Rawlings should have been sitting there pecking on an old Royal typewriter. The structure was draped with moss dangling from two huge oak trees leaning over it like giant hands. The next morning I discovered that it sat quite near a small bay where Ann had fished with her father when she was a child. I also learned that Beecher had never spent a night there. It was Ann's private domain and held its own secrets as well as promises.

"This was my family's summer cottage when I was a child. My father left it to me when he passed away. Beecher kept our home and most of our property, but he wasn't able to get my dad's house. He wanted me to put it in both our names when my dad died, but I refused. I paid for my refusal, but it was worth it in the long run," said Ann. Then she laughed and said, "Oh, I guess you already knew all that. I assume you have read all four diaries?"

"Yes, my dear, I have, and the cottage is lovely! It is exactly as I imagined it would be. This takes me back in time. How long has it been here?" I asked.

"My dad and his father built it the year before I was born, so it has been here sixty-six years. These old Cracker houses seem to hold up well in Florida. It has seen its share of hurricanes and is still solid as a rock, just like me. I've weathered a few storms of my own," said Ann laughing with the innocence of a child.

Ann's childish innocence, however, was tempered by the wisdom of experience. She had the fearless quality of a battle-tested warrior with none of the hardness.

I pulled my bag from the back seat of the car and followed Ann up the steps. Two comfortable rocking chairs on the front porch invited conversation.

Ann unlocked the front door and took my bag then said, "Why don't you have a seat? I'll fix us a cup of coffee and we can talk. I suspect you have a few questions for me." She turned on the little porch lantern, and I watched her search the room for an unseen demon.

"Ann, I have to ask. Has your husband been threatening you. You seem to be looking for something or someone," I commented.

Ann jerked to a normal stance and smiled. "Not really. I suppose I am still a bit jumpy," she replied.

"Have you had any contact with him since the divorce?" I asked.

"Not intentionally," Ann answered. She hesitated. I could see she wanted to say something else. She turned away from me and rummaged through the cupboard until she found the coffee. Her tiny hands were shaking.

"Are you alright? You seem nervous," I said.

"Yes, I'm fine. Beecher followed me most of the way home from church today. I was afraid he might show up at my door, but he turned off before I got to the Indian Pass road. I think he just likes to remind me he's still in my life," Ann explained.

"Is he?" I asked.

"When you share two children and almost fifty years of living together, he is always in your life. There is no escaping him," Ann said. She focused so intently on the coffee pot, her voice was barely audible.

"How do your children feel about all this?" I asked.

She sighed and faced me with her back braced against the counter. "He has convinced them I made up the stories of abuse. They are certain their father would never do such things. They think I have lost my mind. He has manipulated my every move all my adult life. Ann doesn't exist. Mama is whatever Daddy says she is. Mrs. Beckham exists. Ann is dead," she said then she stiffened her back and returned to the coffee pot.

I stood like a statue watching her until she faced me again. I looked into her face and saw a ghost where a woman should be. "Ann," I said, "Do you have a restraining order in place?"

"No, not anymore. It wouldn't do any good. The sheriff is his best buddy. He has also been convinced I am losing my marbles. He feels sorry for me that I have lost such a fine husband," Ann replied.

I sat down heavily on the nearest chair. I thought I was a strong woman, but I suddenly felt powerless to help Ann. She stood at the counter until the coffee pot stopped perking then she poured two cups and sat down across from me. I bit my lip and considered my next words carefully.

"Ann, tomorrow morning I am going to call my assistant and have her contact one of our clients in Tallahassee. He owns a security company. I'm going to have him come down here and install a security system no one can penetrate without your knowing. Your security will be monitored twenty-four hours a day. We are also going to get you a dog and a gun. Do you own a gun?" I asked.

"No, Beecher has a full arsenal, but he kept all of them. He has his own little secret room full of weapons and ammo, but I didn't have the key," Ann said.

I took a deep breath and set my jaw. "Well, that is about to change!" I said.

"I appreciate your concern, Emily. I know you mean well, but I'll be alright. He won't hurt me anymore. And I really can't afford any of that. I have some money my father left me, but not enough for that kind of extravagance. Beecher only gives me enough money each month to barely get by on," said Ann.

My back stiffened and my left eyebrow went up. "I will pay for it," I said. "And soon you will be able to afford it if you will allow me to publish your diaries. Ann, women all over the world need to hear your story. You have far more sisters than you realize. Your story is so common it hurts me to think about it, but women won't talk about it. Will you let me tell your story?"

For a long while Ann looked out the window at the shadowy remnants of Sunday. I felt the battle raging in her head.

The sun had set, but my surroundings were still lit by the end of day. The cabin sat in the center of what I would describe as a copse. It was a small grove of native trees that had been twisted and shaped by countless storms and floods. They stayed low to the ground, away from the constant winds that battered the spit of land called Indian Pass.

Ann looked out into the settling day and sipped her coffee. The odd thing about her pose was that she didn't seem embarrassed by the silence between us. I waited. Finally she said, "So Emily, should I assume that you read *all* my diaries?"

"Every page," I replied. Then I waited. Ann dropped her head as if she were about to pray, but instead, she chuckled.

"You were shocked that I sent them to you, weren't you?" she asked.

Now it was my turn to laugh. "Yes, I suppose that is one way to put it. Normally, I would not even consider reading informal diaries, but something about yours held me in their spell. Are all the stories you told actually true?" I asked.

"Every word," Ann answered. I was surprised at the brevity of her answers given the long flowing entries in the diaries.

"Ann, have you ever published any of your writing?" I asked.

"Not a word. Beecher never wanted me to work,

and he was suspicious of any close relationships I tried to establish, so I was limited to the private pages of my journals. He never knew they existed. I kept them under my mattress, all of them," explained Ann.

"Did you go to college?" I asked.

"No, we got married the year after I graduated from high school. I was working for my father until I decided what I wanted to do then Beecher asked me to marry him. He never wanted me to go to college. He said a wife was supposed to be 'barefoot and pregnant' so I was. Does that sound familiar?" Ann asked. "I never knew if we could afford for me to go to college. He controlled the money. He gave me what he thought I needed and said he would take care of the rest. He told me I didn't need to worry about anything."

I set my empty coffee cup down on the end table and muttered, "Son of a bitch!"

Ann smiled and said, "That pretty much describes him except that his mother was as beaten down as I was. She definitely was not a bitch. He learned his behavior from a good teacher—his father. Maybe we could call him a son of an asshole."

I slouched back in my chair and said, "Yes, I would definitely go along with that. Men learn how to treat women by watching the men in their lives. Sounds like Beecher was a willing student. So does this mean you will agree to publish your diaries?"

"Can you guarantee me anonymity?" Ann asked.

"Do you want anonymity?" I asked.

"I don't know," Ann said.

"Are you afraid of what Beecher will do?" I asked.

"No, there isn't much else he can do to me," Ann replied.

"Then why don't you want anyone to know who you are?" I asked. I knew the answer, but I needed her to know.

"I don't know," Ann said. She shrugged and frowned.

"Are you embarrassed?" I asked.

"I suppose I am," she replied.

"If you will stand tall and tell your story, I promise you I will be there every step of the way. You will be the hero of so many women. You will lead them out into the open so that none of you will have to hide ever again. If you can do that, maybe some of your pain will have been worthwhile," I replied.

She stared out into the darkness and hesitated then said, "Yes, I will release the diaries to you. I will step out of the cave and into the sunshine. I have nothing else to lose. But I must warn you, Beecher may come after you if you help me."

"You let me worry about that. I've wrestled with demons far more powerful than he. If he comes after me, he'll have problems he never even imagined," I said. I quietly hoped he would come after me, but he never did.

We talked most of the night then the next day we went shopping. Work began two days later on installation of a high tech security system. We purchased a stainless steel Smith and Wesson .38 special with a laser sight, and we enrolled Ann in a conceal carry permit class. I paid the instructor to take her to the target range and make sure she could hit the bull's eye—every time. If I had any say in the matter, and I did, she would never take another blow. The one thing I hate most is bullies. My own feelings seeped into my professionalism, and I took it upon myself to destroy this bully, one way or another. Unfortunately, I was not the one holding the weapon, but I now controlled the rights to the ammunition.

We found Ann over the next twelve months, and I found a friend I would treasure forever. What we found most likely surprised Ann, but it was exactly what I expected from the moment I began reading her diaries. Her story began with JT Stanton, her first love.

2
JT STANTON

JT Stanton was a quiet boy. He was tall and blonde with a pleasant smile. He always made the top grades in his class, but no one noticed him—no one except Ann. She smiled at him when she passed him in the hall. At first she thought he didn't like her because he didn't seem to notice, but he did notice. He assumed she was just being polite.

The day before spring break her junior year, he smiled back. He was a senior, and he smiled at her. Ann spent the entire week of spring break thinking about him. Annuals had come out the week before, so she stared for hours at his picture. He was president of the Honor Society and was also in Math Club and Key Club. He had played in the band his freshman year. She wondered what instrument he played. She wondered about everything. She wanted to know all about him. One smile had ignited a fire that would burn for the rest of her life.

When classes resumed after spring break, she made sure she was outside his first class minutes before the bell rang. She saw him coming down the hall. His hair fell just above his eyebrow in a gentle wave, and his blue shirt made his eyes look like a summer sky. She felt her heart beating so fast she was afraid he would notice as he walked toward her.

"Hi," she said to him when he approached her.

"Hi," he said. "I'm JT."

Ann grinned. "Yes, I know," she said.

"But I don't know your name. That's not quite fair, is it?" JT asked.

"Ann, I'm Ann," she said.

"A pretty name for a pretty girl," he said. He gave her that smile again.

"Thank you," Ann said. The bell rang. She said, "Gotta run. See you around?"

"Yes, ma'am. I think you will," JT said with a blue-eyed grin.

Ann was in no hurry to leave campus that day. Her house was only a few blocks from the school, so she walked home after school every day. Her mother was accustomed to her going to the library or visiting with her friends after school, so she didn't have to hurry away from campus. She walked toward the senior parking lot hoping to see JT. He saw her first.

JT walked silently up behind her. He followed her a few steps then whispered, "There's someone following you."

Ann stopped so suddenly JT almost ran into her. She knew his voice instantly. She whispered, "Should I scream for help?"

JT couldn't help himself. He burst out laughing and

stepped around in front of her. "I don't know. Should you?" he asked.

Ann beamed. "I think I'll take a wait-and-see approach. What do you think?" she asked.

JT was facing her and walking backward in front of her. "That sounds reasonable to me. But then I'm not always reasonable," he answered.

Suddenly he stumbled over a traffic cone in the parking lot. "This doesn't seem to be working out well for me. Can you help me out here?" he asked.

Ann grinned and asked, "What exactly can I do to help you out?"

Now JT laughed. "I'm trying to flirt with a pretty girl with a pretty name," he said.

Ann replied, "Well it looks to me like you are doing a pretty good job, but you probably should stop trying to walk backward."

"Ok, good advice. Where are you going?" he asked.

"Home," Ann said.

"Are you looking for your car?" he asked.

"No," Ann replied.

"You aren't helping me much. Let me make this simple: where is home, and how do you intend to get there?" JT continued.

"I give up," Ann said. "Home is three blocks that way and one block that way, and I always walk home."

"Now we are getting somewhere. Do you want to walk beside my car while I follow you, or would you like to get in my car and let me take you home?" JT asked.

"Are those my only two choices?" Ann asked.

"Yes, I believe they are," JT replied. He was

leaning against a little red sports car, and he had a firm set to his gorgeous square jaw.

"Hmmmm," Ann said. "Is this your car?" she asked.

"Yes, ma'am," JT replied.

"Ok, I'll ride," Ann said.

"Oh, so you only love me for my car. Is that it?" JT asked as he scrambled around to the other side to open the door for her.

Ann followed him and sat down in the car. She smoothed her skirt and finally replied, "The jury's still out on that one."

JT grinned and closed the door. "I can wait," he said.

He sat down in the driver's seat and shifted into reverse. When he started to back out, he put his hand on the back of Ann's seat. His hand brushed her shoulder in the process. She tingled from her head to her toes. She thought, "So this is what it is like." She smiled in the sunshine.

The ride home was far too short. When they pulled up in the driveway, her mother was watering the zinnias in the side flowerbed. She wiped her brow and turned off the hose. She walked toward them, looking askance at Ann.

"Mother, this is JT Stanton," Ann said.

Mrs. White pulled off her gloves and slapped them against her leg to knock the dirt off. She was sizing up this young man she had heard nothing about. "I'm pleased to meet you, JT Stanton. I'm Ann's mother. I'd like to say I've heard a lot about you, but I haven't," she said.

JT smiled an awkward smile and replied, "I met Ann before spring break, and I offered her a ride home. I hope that was okay with you," JT said.

"Well, she looks none the worse for it. Would you like to come in? I just baked a batch of oatmeal cookies. They are still hot," Mrs. White said.

JT had been brought up in the South, so he knew better than to refuse. "Sure," he replied. Then he looked at Ann to see if he had done the right thing. Obviously, he had.

Ann took his hand and led him inside. "Come on JT, Mother's cookies are the best," she said. He knew it was more than cookies Ann's mother was thinking about.

Ann and JT sat down at the kitchen table and Mrs. White set a plate of cookies and two glasses of chocolate milk in front of them. She pretended to be tidying up the kitchen for a few minutes then walked out of the room.

Ann and JT talked quietly while they ate the cookies then JT said, "Ann, my mom expects me home soon, so I had better go, but can I drive you home again tomorrow? Better yet, can I pick you up in the morning and drive you to school?"

"Sure, I'd like that," said a very happy girl on a very warm spring day. She walked out to the car with JT as her mother watched from the window. JT took Ann's hand and held it while they stood beside the car. He was nearly a foot taller than she was and had broad shoulders and a contagious smile, none of which was lost on Ann. She kept looking up at him hoping he would lean down and kiss her, but he didn't. Finally he got in the car and cranked the engine. Ann put her hand on his shoulder and said, "So I'll see you in the morning?"

"Yes, ma'am, you will," he replied.

It took Ann two hours to decide what she wanted to

wear the next morning. She finally decided on her red and white sundress with spaghetti straps that tied in neat bows over each shoulder. JT's car was racing red, so she thought that had to be the right choice. Apparently it was.

Ann was waiting on the front porch when JT drove up the next morning. She was down the front steps and across the yard before he could get out of the car, but he bounded out in time to run around and open the door for her. He held her hand and looked at her as she sat down. "You look beautiful in that dress—no wait, you are beautiful, dress or no dress. Oh, crap! That's not what I meant to say!" he stammered.

Ann laughed and said, "Thank you, I think."

"You know I meant that as a compliment, don't you?" JT asked.

"Yes, I do," said Ann with the softest smile JT had ever seen. The world stood still for them that moment as they looked at each other sitting in the sunshine with the top down in the little red car.

When he recovered his composure, JT said, "Wheew! I just meant that you are beautiful but the dress is pretty too, or something like that. Do you have this affect on all the guys?" he asked.

"There are no *guys*!" Ann said.

"Are you kidding me? There are no guys in your life?" JT asked.

"JT, I don't go out much. My parents are pretty strict. I haven't had any real boyfriends. I spend my time with my family and my friend, Nell," Ann answered.

"Oh, do you think your parents would let you go out with me, that is if you want to?" JT asked.

"The answer is yes, and yes. I'd like to go out with you, and my mother liked you. She's a very good judge of character," Ann explained.

"Would you like to go out Friday night? Maybe to a movie?" JT asked.

"Sure," said Ann, trying very hard to hide her excitement.

Soon they were at school and JT pulled into the parking lot. Three of his friends watched as he walked around to open the door for Ann. They rolled their eyes and made unheard comments to each other. Ann and JT walked side-by-side down the sidewalk unaware of the other students milling around them.

By the time they got to the door of Ann's classroom, she knew JT had been accepted to the University of Florida for the fall term. He would be leaving town, so she would not be able to see him on a regular basis. He was a serious student who wanted to go to medical school, so he had years of intense study ahead of him. She assumed a girlfriend was not high on his list of priorities. Still she was elated just to stand beside him.

JT put his hand on the small of her back and said, "Have a good day, Ann. I'll see you at the car after school."

Nell walked up about that time. Her mouth dropped open, and when JT was out of earshot, she asked, "Who is that? And where did he come from?"

They walked into class and Ann said, "I'll tell you later."

Nell was stunned. She knew every move Ann made, and she had no idea how this happened without her knowing. But it obviously had.

As soon as the bell rang, she was at Ann's side asking questions. Ann tried to brush it off as nothing remarkable, but Nell took one look at Ann's face and knew that was not true. Still, she got no real answers from Ann. She didn't realize Ann really had no answers to give at this point.

After what seemed like an eternity, Friday night arrived. Ann finally had her chance to get to know JT.

The little red MG pulled up in Ann's driveway promptly at 7:00. JT walked up to the door and rang the doorbell. Mr. White opened the door immediately to find JT holding a small bouquet of flowers. Ann was standing behind her dad when he opened the door, so he turned to her and said, "Oh, look, Ann. This young man has brought me some flowers, and they are my favorites." Mr. White looked so serious JT almost handed him the flowers.

Ann playfully pushed her dad aside and said, "Pay no attention to him. He's my daddy—he's obligated to be silly," Ann said.

JT smiled and looked from Ann to her father and back again. He held the flowers out between them as if he wasn't sure who to give them to. Ann took them from him and said, "Thank you, JT. They are lovely. Did you know that daisy's are my favorite flowers?"

"No, I didn't. Are these daisies? I sure hope they are," JT answered.

They all laughed and Ann tucked her arm under his. "Daddy, this is JT. Now shoo..." Ann said.

"Come in, JT. I'll just be a minute. I want to put the flowers in a vase so they will still be beautiful when I get home. I'll put them beside my bed so I can see them every time I wake up during the night," Ann said.

"Sure," JT said. Then he looked at her father.

"Mr. White, it is nice to meet you. Your daughter is a very special girl. I promise I will take good care of her," JT said.

"That would be wise, son. You see, she is my only daughter, so I take her welfare very seriously. Guard her life like you would your own—because your life just might depend on her safety," Mr. White said.

"Yes, sir! I will do that," JT said. A heavy silence fell between them, unbroken until Ann crossed from the kitchen through the hall and into her bedroom. JT smiled when she opened her bedroom door, and he saw inside. It was just as he had imagined it to be, pink and white with lace and ribbons all over. It suited her very well. He thought it was fitting for an angel.

Ann flounced out the door, looking like a fairytale princess. Her light brown hair had a hint of red in it, and she had pulled it up into a ponytail that bounced when she walked. JT's heart skipped a beat when she reached for his arm and said, "Let's go, Lancelot."

They drove away from Ann's house that night with stars in their eyes and dreams in their hearts.

JT handed the lady in the ticket booth three dollars in exchange for two tickets. He let out the clutch and the car eased into the lane. They parked near the back row of the tiers of drive-in parking, and JT lifted the speaker from its rack and hung it on the slightly raised window. The previews had just begun. They came to see *The Last Picture Show*.

"I've heard this is a really good movie, but it is

sad," JT said.

"Yes, I've heard the same thing. I'm sure we will enjoy it," said Ann.

Then Ann said, "I'm just happy I get to see it with you."

JT smiled and put his arm around her. "Me too," he answered.

"Ann, there's a smudge on your nose," JT said.

"Oh, where?" asked Ann as she rubbed her nose.

JT took her face in his hands and said, "Let me see. I'll get it." Then he grinned and kissed her nose. "Sorry, but I've been wanting to do that since the first time I saw you."

"Me too," said Ann. She snuggled as close as the gear shift would allow her. MG's are not made for snuggling. But JT put his arm around her and pressed his face against hers.

"You smell so good," he said.

"Thank you," said Ann. She turned her face to his and waited. He looked at her for an eternity then tenderly kissed her. "You know we have to watch this movie, don't you?" Ann asked timidly.

"Yes, it's just hard for me to see the screen when I'm looking at you," he said.

Ann clutched his hand and said, "JT, tell me who you are."

"What do you mean?" he asked.

"Tell me about your family, about your goals in life, about your favorite color," I want to know all about you," Ann said.

"I thought you wanted to watch the movie," JT teased.

"I have two eyes and two ears. I'll use one of each for the movie and reserve the other ones for you," Ann replied, but it was clear even to JT that she was far more interested in him than the movie.

"Well, I am the youngest of four children. My brothers are married and my sister is a senior in college. I've lived here all my life, and I am going to the University of Florida in August," said JT. "Does that answer your questions?"

"That's a nice start. Are you really going to med school," Ann asked.

"That's the plan, but who knows if I will make it. There are lots of chances for slips between here and there," replied JT.

"Something tells me you won't slip. Why do you want to be a doctor? That's a lot of hard work," said Ann.

"I've wanted to be a doctor as long as I could remember. My sister was very ill when I was four years old. She was eight. She had spinal meningitis. We almost lost her. We took her to Shands Hospital at the University of Florida and they saved her life. I was so frightened because I loved her so much, and I was afraid of losing her. Those doctors are my heroes, so I want to be one of them. I want to specialize in pediatrics and save children like my sister," JT explained.

"Oh, no! Is she ok now?" Ann asked.

"Yes, she is fine. She is finishing up a degree in engineering at Georgia Tech. We are still very close. You will like her. But I warn you, she is very different from you," said JT.

Ann backed away from him, "Oh, she's different,

and you love her very much…hmmmm. What does that tell me?" she said.

JT laughed and replied, "No, not in a bad way. In a good way. I wouldn't want to date a girl like my sister, but I love her very much. She's too feisty for me. You'll like her though. She's so headstrong she follows her own rules. If you play in her game, you have to play by her rules. I've never been one to give orders—maybe she's the reason. She orders us all around. When a girl can keep three brothers in line, she's got something special. I just wouldn't want to be married to her."

"Oh, I see. I can't wait to meet her," said Ann, but she wasn't at all sure she meant it.

"Now, how about you? I don't know anything about you except that you are beautiful and you like daisies," said JT.

"I'm an only child. Maybe a little bit sheltered. My life pretty much consists of church and school. We belong to the First Baptist Church, where both of my parents sing in the choir. I play the piano for the children's choir. I want to go to college, but I'm not sure where I will go yet or even what I want to do with my life. I've grown up thinking I'd be someone's wife and raise a family, but compared to you, that doesn't sound like much of a goal," said Ann.

JT suddenly became very serious and wrinkles creased his forehead. He replied, "That doesn't sound like much of a goal? Ann, that's the highest goal there is. That's what my mother has dedicated her life to. Don't ever be ashamed of wanting to be a wife and mother. You are beautiful and smart, but most of all you are good and true.

Never lose sight of who you are. You are the best life has to offer. Any man worth his salt could see that."

Ann was stunned. She looked at him without saying a word. She didn't know what to say. Finally she said quietly, "You really think so?"

JT closed his eyes and whispered, "I know so." He leaned over and held her face in his hands while he kissed her. She wrapped her arms around him and nestled her face against his. Their hearts pounded in synchronized rhythm.

It would be many years before JT would know what his words meant in her life, but he never forgot and neither did she. He would repeat them more than once over a lifetime of love and loss.

They didn't see much of the movie, but they knew this was the beginning of something that even time could not erase. When they pulled into Ann's driveway that night, JT turned the car off and looked at Ann's face in the moonlight.

"Ann, I want to ask you something," he said.

"Sure, JT. What is it?" she replied.

"Would you go to the prom with me? I've never been to any of the dances because I never knew anyone I'd like to dance with, but I'd like to dance with you. Will you go with me? It is the last chance for me. I'll be out of here when this year ends," JT kept explaining until Ann interrupted him.

"Yes, yes. I would love to dance with you," she said.

Ann and her mother spent hours making a dress. It was a confection of pink tulle and lace over delicate white silk. The bodice was fitted and the skirt flared with layer upon layer of shimmering fabric. When J.T arrived to pick her up, he was stunned. He had never seen anything so beautiful in his life. He wore a black tuxedo with a rose cummerbund. For his lapel, Ann had a deep rose boutonnière to match the pink rose corsage he brought for her. She pinned the flower on his lapel and her mother fastened the corsage to her gown. They posed obediently for her mother to take pictures then walked out the door. Her parents stood on the porch watching as they drove away.

  JT had brought his mother's car that night. He guessed that her gown would not fit in the little red MG. He was correct. He helped her into the car and stood looking at her until she finally said, "What? What's wrong?"

  JT smiled and said, "Nothing is wrong. Everything is perfect. You are perfect." Then he closed the door and went around to the driver's door. He took a deep breath and got in beside his princess. Ann slid over as close to him as she could. She leaned her head on his shoulder. He put his arm around her, and they drove away into the future.

3
SENIOR YEAR

After a short summer of hot Florida nights with JT, Ann's senior year began without him. JT left for Gainesville the week before, leaving Ann in tears. Nell walked with her to class and tried to distract her with chatter, but Ann stared silently at her steps on the concrete floor.

"Ann, come on, this is the first day of our senior year. It will be the best year of our lives," Nell urged.

"I hope it will be your best year, Nell, but it won't be mine. JT is on a huge college campus with gorgeous coeds all around him. He'll find someone else; I know he will," said Ann.

"Hogwash! He can't even see anyone but you. If you could see the way he looks at you, you would know that. You are so blind! Good grief—you are hopeless! I give up. Just don't ask me to become a nun because you have. Janie is having a party Saturday night at her house, and I'll be there with or without you," said Nell.

"I'm sorry, Nell. JT might call this weekend. Anyway, I am just not in a party mood. You go and have fun," said Ann.

"Your loss," said Nell as she went into her classroom and shut the door behind her.

Saturday night came and Ann was true to her answer. She was at home sitting beside the phone when JT called. He was missing her as much as she was missing him. When they hung up, Ann cried herself to sleep.

Nell, however, was at Janie's party. She had met the man she would eventually marry. Buddy was Janie's cousin who lived across town and worked at the local hardware store on weekends and on a construction crew during the week. He had dreams of becoming a successful home builder. He was handsome in a rugged sort of way, and Nell was definitely interested. They danced all night and went out for a late night supper when everyone else went home. Janie and Buddy's friend went with them.

Buddy's friend was Beecher Beckham. He was short and stocky and reminded Nell of a shorter and more muscular version of Elvis Presley. Janie didn't seem too interested, but she went along anyway. Half way through his burger, Beecher asked Nell about her friend, Ann.

"Nell, aren't you and Ann White friends?" Beecher asked.

"Yes, why?" Nell asked with a frown.

"Just wondered," he said.

"And why did you wonder?" asked Nell rather pointedly.

"Oh, I don't know. I thought I might ask her out sometime," said Beecher.

Janie glared at him. She thought it took nerve to ask about another girl when your date was sitting beside you, but then she realized it wasn't a real date. It had been, but suddenly it wasn't.

Nell cocked her head to the side and gave him *the look* then replied, "Don't bother. She won't go out with you." She should never have said that to Beecher Beckham. The only thing larger than his pickup truck was his ego.

Beecher laughed and said, "Want to bet?"

"Sure, I'll bet on that. She's very much in love. She's not looking for a boyfriend. You'll see," said Nell.

"Why don't you give me her phone number and we'll see about that," said Beecher.

"Not a chance in hell!" replied Nell. Then she said, "Buddy, I think I'd like to go home now."

"Sure, Nell. Let's go. We'll see you two later," Buddy said to Janie and Beecher.

Janie and Beecher looked at each other, wondering what had triggered that response. Before they could react, Buddy picked up the check and was at the register paying the bill.

Buddy put his arm around Nell, and they walked out the door. Beecher could tell from the expression on Nell's face that she was not happy. She nodded toward him and Buddy whispered something to her. "What a jerk," said Beecher.

"What do you mean, Beecher?" asked Janie.

"I know he's your cousin, and he's my friend, but sometimes he's a real jerk. He thinks I can't get a date with Ann. I'll show them both," said Beecher.

The next day Beecher showed up at the First Baptist

Church. He conveniently sat behind Ann so that she would have to walk by him on her way out. She did.

When the service was over and people began to leave, he slid over next to the aisle and waited. When Ann was beside him, he stood up suddenly and bumped into her. "Oh, excuse me," he said.

Ann looked at him and smiled. "It's ok," she said and kept walking. Beecher followed her. When they got outside the door, Ann stopped to wait for her parents.

Ann wore a white eyelet dress and white polished heels. Around her neck was a small strand of pearls, which matched her delicate single pearl earrings. Beecher thought she looked like an angel. He was hooked.

He turned to her and said, "I don't think we've met. My name is Beecher Beckham. Aren't you Nell's friend?"

"Yes, I am. Do you know Nell?" asked Ann politely.

"Yes, she's dating my friend Buddy," Beecher said.

"Oh, that's nice," said Ann. She stepped off the sidewalk to look for her parents. "Nice to meet you. I have to go find my parents," Ann said. She hurried away down the sidewalk hoping to see her parents coming out of the annex door. Something about Beecher made her uncomfortable.

Beecher watched Ann walk away. He smiled. He sauntered out to his truck and got in, but he didn't drive away immediately. He watched Ann link arms with her father and walk to their car. He surreptitiously followed them home and noted where she lived. The next Sunday, he showed up at church again. By Christmas, he had joined the congregation.

Ann waited not so patiently for Christmas break. JT had been home only once during the semester, and then he had so many family activities and class projects to work on, Ann felt like she had hardly seen him when he left again. Even Thanksgiving dinner seemed a stretch for him.

He was anxious about grades and eager to return to Gainesville. He always seemed tense and worried. If he could maintain the perfect 4.0, he would almost be assured of getting into medical school. His GPA appeared to be more important to him than she was. She was seventeen, and she felt neglected. She began to wonder if she still had a place in his life.

They exchanged letters every week but JT's had become shorter and shorter. Her head understood that he was trying to keep his grades up, but her heart failed to get the message.

JT arrived for Christmas a week before Ann's school break began. He showed up at her door just before dinner. She thought he would not arrive until the next day, so when he knocked on the door, she assumed it was the paper boy collecting for the daily newspaper.

Ann opened the door and looked up. She saw his face and screamed, "JT, you're home!" She jumped into his arms.

He picked her up and swung her around. When he put her down, they stood there holding onto each other until Ann's mother called out, "Who is it dear?" She had talked to JT's mother and knew very well who it was.

The two of them walked into the kitchen arm in arm. "Welcome home, JT. How is school?" Mrs. White asked.

"It's much better from a distance. I'm happy to be home," JT said.

"And to see me?" Ann asked.

"Oh, I guess so," JT teased. Ann poked him in the ribs.

"Mother, can JT stay for dinner?" Ann asked.

"Who do you think that extra plate is for? Phoebe called me earlier today and told me JT was home, so I'm a step ahead of you two," Ann's mother said.

"Mother, why didn't you tell me?" Ann scolded.

"And spoil his surprise? Never!" she replied. Ann's mother and father had come to look at JT as part of their family. They believed he would be someday.

JT laughed and said, "Thanks, Mrs. White. The look on Ann's face was worth a million dollars. I don't get to shock her very often."

Dinner with Ann's family unfolded as naturally as if he had always been there. JT stayed until midnight and left Ann with stars in her eyes.

On Christmas day, JT attended church with Ann. This fact was not lost on Beecher. He sat behind them and watched their every move. He had no claim on Ann; he had not even asked her out—yet. He was biding his time. But still he was insanely jealous. He was more determined than ever. Buddy planned to give Nell an engagement ring for Christmas, and he hadn't even asked Ann for a date. He was waiting to make sure that when he did ask, she would say yes. JT was one of those "college boys," so Beecher had to play his cards carefully to unseat the king.

On Christmas morning, JT gave Ann a small gold lavalier with his fraternity symbol on it. She wore it around her neck that morning and clung to JT's arm. She was happy.

For New Years Eve, JT took Ann out to dinner. He wore a black suit with a festive red tie. He stood at Ann's door with a small corsage in his hand and knocked on the door. Ann opened the door and took JT's breath away. She stood like a vision in front of him. Her dress was black velvet and had a short gold satin jacket, which she held in her hand. The dress hugged her curves in all the right places, making JT want to run his hands over every inch of it. He was speechless. He had never seen her dressed like this. The girl he had met in the hall at school was a woman standing in front of him on the most festive night of the year, and she was his.

Ann held the door with cold air blowing in. She shivered and said, "Aren't you going to come in?"

JT woke from his dream and smiled. "Oh, yes, I am. I'm in shock because you are so beautiful!" he said.

They both laughed and Ann said, "Right answer! Thank you. You look pretty nice, yourself. Would you like to take me out?"

"Yes, ma'am, I believe I would," JT said. He handed her the corsage, a single red rose tied with gold ribbon.

"Thank you! I love it. Help me with my jacket and we'll pin it on," Ann said.

JT took the small black jacket in his hands and held it for her to slip her arms into the sleeves. He felt the cool, smooth satin lining. It slid effortlessly over her arms, and JT paused as he smoothed its creases. He felt the warmth of her skin and the curve of her neck. He wanted to take her in his arms and hold her close to his body, but that would have to wait.

 JT closed his eyes and took a deep breath. "Girl, you have no idea what you do to me," he whispered.

 Ann smiled and took his hand.

 Ann's mother came into the room with her camera and said, "No one leaves this room until I take a picture."

 JT put his arm around Ann and beamed. Ann looked up at him with a soft smile. It was the image Ann would hold in her mind for the rest of her life.

 As they sat at the restaurant on the last night of the year JT met Ann, he kept gazing at her as if she were a mirage and might vaporize if he blinked. He knew he wanted to spend the rest of his life with her, but he also grasped the reality of that plan. Ann was oblivious to the workings of his mind that night and was deliriously happy to be with him. They danced until midnight and held onto each other as if life would end with the sunrise.

 Ann's happiness was short lived, however. The night before JT returned to Gainesville, he took Ann to a secluded park and said he wanted to talk to her.

 JT brushed off the surface of a stone park bench. The stone was cold, and he shivered. "Sit here with me," he said.

 He looked at Ann's face and saw confusion. "Ann," he said and paused, "I will be away most of next semester. The only time I will be home is for spring break. It isn't fair for me to ask you to stay home all the time. I can't be here to take you to your senior prom. I know how special that was for me, and I'm sure it is to you. I don't want you to miss that experience. I have to keep my grades up if I'm going to get into medical school, but I can't ask you to miss out on your senior year because of me. I love you enough to let you be free. If you want to go out with someone else, I don't want to stop you."

Ann's eyes filled with tears, and she asked, "JT, are you breaking up with me?"

"No, no, Ann. I love you, but I want you to enjoy your senior year. I probably have ten long years of school in front of me before I can get married. That's a long time for you to wait. That isn't fair to you," JT explained.

Ann stood up and walked away from him. He followed her and stood behind her in the darkness. He put his arms around her and rocked back and forth. She was crying quietly.

She whispered, "Don't you think I should get to decide what is best for me?"

"Of course, I do. That is what I'm saying. You should be able to do what you want to. I don't want to stand in your way. Being tied to me for ten years while I struggle though medical school, internship, and residency would be no life for you. You deserve better," JT said.

"You've met someone else, haven't you?" Ann asked.

"No, no! Of course not! Is that what you really think?" asked JT.

Ann faced JT and said, "I don't know what to think anymore!" She walked away from him.

JT followed her and caught her by the shoulders. "Ann, stop. Don't do this, please. I'm only trying to be fair. Do you really want to wear an engagement ring for ten years and try to explain that to everyone?"

"If that's what it takes to hold onto you, I do!" Ann said.

JT folded her in his arms and said, "I love you, and I always will. That's the only thing I know for sure today."

They walked back to his car without saying another word. Something was broken and Ann thought it would never be the same again. JT had doubts, and he had somehow transferred those doubts to her shoulders. He never doubted his love for her, but he questioned the future. When they got in the car, Ann sat on her side as far away from JT as she could. They passed several cars and one pickup truck on the way to Ann's house. The truck belonged to Beecher Beckham. He saw where Ann was sitting.

The following Sunday, Beecher moved up a row. He entered the sanctuary early and sat on the pew where Ann always sat. Ann walked into the sanctuary and to the customary pew. She saw Beecher and hesitated, but there was no graceful way to avoid sitting beside him.

When she sat down, Beecher whispered, "Hi! Did you have a nice Christmas?"

"Yes, it was fine," Ann replied. She said nothing else and picked up the hymnal searching for the first hymn of the day.

Beecher did the same, but he smiled. Ann did not. When the congregation stood to sing the first hymn, Beecher held the book in front of him and sang with the most beautiful voice Ann had ever heard. His voice was a deep baritone and his diction clear and melodious. She had never noticed his voice before.

When the service was over, Ann said, "Beecher,

you have a beautiful voice. You should join the choir."

"Thank you, but I enjoy sitting out here beside you," he said and pretended to be joking.

Ann smiled and said, "No, I'm serious. You really should sing with the choir."

Beecher returned her smile and said, "I was serious, too." He walked behind her and into the sunshine. Ann had never really paid any attention to him before, but she realized he was actually quite handsome and very different from JT.

Ann and Beecher were still talking when Ann's parents walked up. "Mom, Dad, this is Beecher. He has a beautiful voice. I was just telling him he should sing with the choir. You really should hear him," Ann insisted.

Ann's father said, "Is that right, young man? We need some young voices to join us. Come over here and let me introduce you to our choir director. Hey, Alice, come meet this young man. Ann thinks he has just the voice we've been looking for."

Alice shook Beecher's hand and said, "Were you sitting near the front?"

Beecher replied, "Yes, ma'am. On the third row beside Ann."

"I heard you. You do have a lovely voice. We need a strong baritone. Would you come to practice Wednesday night? We'd love to have you join us," Alice said.

"Oh, I don't know. I never thought about singing in a choir. I don't have any training. I just sing to be singing," Beecher explained. He realized the choir was his opportunity to see Ann and for her to see him in the *right* light. "Sure, I'll give it a try. Why not?" he said. He looked at Ann and raised his eyebrows as if he were taken aback.

When Wednesday came, Beecher was the star of choir practice. His voice stood out. Everyone knew he was an asset to the group. They treated him like royalty. The following Sunday, Beecher wore a gold robe and stood beside Ann's father. He smiled. He was *in*.

After church Ann waited for her parents, but when they came out the door, they were not alone. Beecher was tagging along beside them.

Beecher followed them to Ann. Mr. White said, "Ann, I'm sure you heard Beecher. His voice is amazing. I'm certainly glad you pointed him out to us. He will be singing solos by Easter."

"Yes, I heard him. He really does have a lovely voice," said Ann. She was moving toward their car and trying to keep distance between herself and Beecher, but he was making it difficult.

Suddenly Mrs. White said, "Beecher, we're going out for lunch. Would you like to join us, our treat?"

Ann shivered.

"Sure, I'd like that very much. Where are you going? I'll meet you there," Beecher said.

"Meet us at the Brown Derby. We'll wait outside for you," said Mr. White.

"Sure. See you there. Oh, Ann, would you like to ride with me?" Beecher asked as if it were an aside.

Ann hurried toward her parents' car. She called over her shoulder, "Thanks, but I'll go with my parents. See you there."

When she got in the car, she scolded her mother, "Mom, why did you do that? I don't want to go out with him. I love JT. I don't want to date Beecher!"

"Honey, it isn't a date. I just thought it would be a nice gesture to treat him to lunch. He is such a nice addition to our choir, and you know what a hard time we have recruiting people to sing with us. No one seems to have time for that anymore. He's not going to interfere with your relationship with JT; besides, he's a very nice boy. JT is going to be gone for a long time. Lots of things can happen between now and then," warned Mrs. White.

Ann closed her eyes and sighed. She kept them closed for several minutes to prevent the tears from rolling down her cheeks. Too soon they arrived at the Brown Derby.

Beecher arrived first and was waiting on the sidewalk when Mr. White pulled into the parking space. Beecher stepped off the curb and stood beside Ann's door, waiting to open it for her. He opened the door and held out his hand to her. She ignored his hand and got out of the car. She smiled a curt smile and said, "Thank you."

Beecher followed them inside and sat opposite Ann at the table. After they had ordered their meals, Mr. White asked, "Beecher, what type work do you do?"

"I'm learning the construction trade with my friend, Buddy. We plan to open our own company when we can save up enough money. We work as many hours as we can and already have a good start toward opening a business. We don't think it will take us too long to get started. We are both studying to take the contractor's exam," Beecher answered.

"Well, that sounds like a fine goal, son. I'm sure you will do well. We are just getting into a building boom.

There are new houses going up all over town," replied Ann's father.

"Yes, sir. We are working on three right now. We've been working twelve-hour days and some weekends, too. It's hard work, but good for our pocketbook," said Beecher.

"You will go far. Keep up the good work. Ann hasn't decided yet what she wants to do. Have you, Ann?" Mr. White said.

"No," replied Ann. She focused on her lunch and refused to look at either of them. Her parents continued to engage in conversation with Beecher, but Ann remained silent. She was relieved when the waitress finally brought the check.

Mr. White put his hand on Beecher's shoulder when they were leaving and said, "Son, I'm really pleased to have you singing with us. Will we see you at practice on Wednesday night?"

"Yes, sir. I'll be there," Beecher answered. Then he added, "Ann, I look forward to seeing you Sunday."

Ann nodded and got in the car. As soon as her father closed the door, it started. "Ann, you don't have to be rude. You could have at least made conversation with Beecher. He is a nice young man, and he was our guest. I didn't ask you to marry him. I simply thought it was a nice gesture to invite him to lunch."

Mrs. White chimed in, "Ann, dear, you must be polite sometimes when you don't particularly like someone. Good manners don't hurt anyone or cost us a dime."

"Yes, Mother," said Ann. She continued to watch the cars pass them. She had nothing else to say. She could only think of JT's last words to her. She wondered what he was doing at the moment. Was he studying, or was he out with some other girl? Her head knew the answer, but her heart wasn't sure.

When Ann's parents came home from choir practice on Wednesday, all they could talk about was Beecher Beckham. Apparently he was their golden boy. They seemed to have rapidly adopted him as the son they never had. On Sunday, he stood beside her father in his gold robe and looked as saintly as he could. He was a full head shorter than her father, but she admitted to herself that he was actually quite handsome. She smiled at him in spite of herself.

Beecher came out of the annex after church with her parents. He stopped by her side and said, "You look very pretty today, Ann, but then you look very pretty every day. Did you enjoy the music today?"

"Yes, I did. I hear you are going to sing a solo next month," Ann said.

"That's what they tell me. We'll see," said Beecher.

"I'm sure it will be beautiful," Ann answered.

"Well, I'll see you next Sunday. I have to go to work now. Buddy is at the jobsite now, and if I don't show up soon, he'll come looking for me," Beecher said. He walked away toward his truck, but when he got there, he turned around and looked at Ann one last time. He smiled and got in his truck.

Ann smiled back.

"Yes!" said Beecher as he drove away.

The following Sunday, Beecher loitered after church and stopped Ann. "Ann, would you go for a ride with me? I'd like to show you the house Buddy and I are working on. Mr. Chambers is giving us more freedom at work, and we are really proud of this one. I'd just like to show it to you. I think you would really like it. It is out by Smith Lake."

Ann looked at her mother, and Mrs. White said, "Go ahead Ann. I'm sure you will enjoy seeing Beecher's work. Smith Lake is a beautiful community. Relax for a change and go have fun."

Ann looked at her mother and back at Beecher then said, "Ok. I have a lot of homework to do, but if we don't stay too long, I'd like to go."

Beecher walked her to his truck and held the door for her. It was a big step up, so he held her hand as she climbed in. She looked around and noted that his truck was completely clean and even the notes tucked behind the visor were neatly arranged. Nothing seemed to be left to chance.

When they drove away from the church, Ann looked back at her parents. They were getting into their car. Her mother waved and smiled. Ann smiled back, but her smile was blank.

Beecher said, "Ann, have you ever been to Smith Lake?"

"No, I haven't," Ann replied.

"It isn't a large lake, but it is spring fed, so it is crystal clear and the lots around it have huge oak and magnolia trees. It is one of my favorite places. I hope to be able to build a house there soon," Beecher said.

"Really? Isn't it quite a ways out of town?" Ann asked.

"Yes, it is a thirty minute drive, but it is worth it. I like to hunt and fish, so it doesn't seem like a long drive to me. I like the isolation. The lots are large, so you really don't have close neighbors," Beecher replied.

"Oh," said Ann. "I like my neighbors. I can't imagine living out of town like that."

"Just wait. I think you will like it when you see it. This house we are building now is a modern version of a Frank Lloyd Wright design. It faces the lake, and the view is spectacular. You can fish from your front yard. I'd like that," Beecher said.

Ann smiled and didn't say anything. They rode along quietly for a few minutes. Beecher turned the radio on, and they listened to music. Beecher sang along with some of the songs. Ann was reminded of what a beautiful voice he had. The conversation turned to music then Beecher put on his blinker, and Ann saw the sign: Smith Lake Village.

They turned down a clay road and bumped along until Ann saw what appeared to be a new house. Only the landscaping told her it was not quite complete. Mounds of sand and several pallets of sod sat behind the house. Beecher stopped the truck just inside what would become the driveway.

"This is it. What do you think?" Beecher asked.

Ann loved what she saw. The sharp angles of the roof pointed to walls of windows with clean lines and colors that blended seamlessly with the surroundings. The windows reflected the brilliant blues of the sky and water. The roof barely broke the plane of the sky, and the lake in front of the house extended the view into infinity. "It is beautiful, Beecher. And you built this?" she asked.

"I wish!" he said. "I had a part in building it. Come inside and let me show you some of my contributions to the construction. Buddy and I did the finish carpentry. We built walls of bookshelves and trimmed the doors and walls."

Beecher lifted the cover on the electrical panel and took out a key then unlocked the back door. When he opened the door, Ann could see straight through to the lake. "Beecher, I'm stunned. This is gorgeous. I love it," she said. She couldn't contain her enthusiasm.

The walls and ceiling were finished with pine tongue and groove boards that had been aged so that the whole room had a calm blue-gray cast. Two sides of the room were glass, and a massive deck extended out twenty feet or more. Because the lot sloped down to the water, the deck seemed to float above the lake.

Ann walked toward the deck as if drawn by a magnet. Beecher stood just inside the door and watched her. She walked over to the wall of glass and stood mesmerized by the view. The deep carpet on the floor muffled his steps, so she didn't hear him walking up behind her. He stood near enough to smell her perfume, but not close enough to touch her.

"Do you like it?" Beecher asked softly.

Ann faced him and saw a different person. He looked at her eyes when he said, "Your opinion is important to me. I wanted you to see what I could do. Do you like what you see?"

Ann was uneasy. She looked back at the lake and answered, "Of course, I do. You've done a fine job." She stepped away from him, uneasy with the space between them. Beecher stepped back also.

"Come in here, Ann. Let me show you the rest of the house," Beecher said. He was standing in the kitchen. He seemed to have transported himself magically to another room. Ann was unaware of her surroundings and confused. She looked at him and tried to smile.

Beecher ran his hand across the grain of the solid slab of sinker cypress used as a countertop. "This wood was harvested locally. It is sinker cypress."

Ann walked over to the kitchen cautiously. "What is sinker cypress? The grain is beautiful. It looks alive."

"Yes, it does. Sinker cypress is from a cypress tree that was felled years ago and left in the river. Bruner Saw Mill has a permit to harvest a certain number of the sinkers each year. The deep reds and yellows in the wood come from the effect of the acid in the water on the wood over many years. It is very durable but expensive. It is one of the things I hope to use in my house. Of course, my house won't be this fancy," said Beecher. He was careful not to move closer to Ann. She was like a kitten one entices with a bowl of milk but dares not reach for. Patience wins that battle.

"That hallway leads to the bedrooms and bathrooms. The master bedroom is especially nice," Beecher said. He left it up to Ann to decide whether she wanted to see them.

"I'm sure it is, but I really need to get back to town. I have some studying I need to do this afternoon," replied Ann.

"Sure," said Beecher. He would wait. He walked back to the door they had first entered and held it open for

Ann. She walked outside and drew her sweater around her shoulders. She shivered when the cold wind hit her face. It was February. The first hint of spring had come, but this day was chilled. The wind blew off the lake and swept her hair across her face like a cowl.

Beecher opened the door of his truck and held out his hand to help Ann get in, but she held onto the doorframe instead. He noticed the gold lavaliere around her neck. She sat down and smoothed her skirt but did not look at Beecher as he got in and put the key in the ignition. He started back out on the clay road and asked, "Well, what do you think?"

Lost in her own thoughts, Ann was startled by his voice. She shook her head and asked, "About what?'

Beecher chuckled and replied, "About the house and about Smith Lake."

"Oh, it's very nice. I like it, and the lake is gorgeous. I'm not sure I'd like to live here though. It seems too far from town for me," Ann replied.

"Really, I'd love to live here. I think it would be nice to have breakfast out on that deck on a sunny day like today. The wind doesn't bother me. I like being outside when it is a little chilly. I could build a fireplace to keep us warm," he said and laughed.

Ann shivered again. "Beecher, I have a boyfriend. I don't want you to get the wrong idea."

"Yes, ma'am. I understand. Where is he, by the way?" Beecher asked pointedly.

Ann looked at him and raised her eyebrow. "He's in Gainesville at the University of Florida," she answered.

"Oh," said Beecher. He turned the music up and

drove on.

Ann got a letter from JT the next day. He was warm and friendly as if nothing had happened, but he didn't sign his letter as he had all the others. He merely wrote, "Thinking of you, JT." There was no "Love, JT."

Ann held the letter in her hand and walked to the window. She stood looking out into the blue sky until she heard her mother's voice calling her to dinner. She laid the letter face down on her desk. After dinner, she sat down at her desk and tried to write a letter to JT. After tossing the first five drafts into the trash can, she gave up.

Two weeks later, Beecher asked her out to lunch after church. She accepted.

4
CAROUSELS AND FERRIS WHEELS

Easter Sunday was their third date. Beecher asked Ann if he could take her to a sunrise service being held at Smith Lake. The little village growing up around the lake had a pavilion with benches facing the sunrise over the lake. He wanted Ann to see the lake as he did. She accepted.

Ann stared at her image in the mirror before the sun rose on Easter Sunday. The lamp on her dressing table cast a small shadow on the wall where an 8x10 framed photo blocked its light. She straightened a curl dangling over her shoulder and blotted her lipstick then picked up the small white clutch lying on her bed. She opened the bag to put her compact and lipstick inside and saw a small picture of herself with JT. They had taken the picture the summer before when her world was a smaller place. They lived one summer in the confines of their hearts, but somehow the world they thought they understood had become far more complex. She snapped the clasp on the purse and listened to the echo of the sound. She stood like a statue for a few seconds then opened the door and walked out to meet Beecher.

Beecher hesitated to ring the doorbell since the sun had not yet risen. He tapped gently on the door. Mrs. White opened it promptly.

"Good morning, Mrs. White. Happy Easter," said Beecher as he handed her a bouquet of white lilies. In his other hand he carried a small octagonal box.

Ann was standing at the top of the stairs dressed in a pale pink linen sheath. She wore the same strand of pearls she had been wearing the first time he saw her. He smiled broadly as he watched her descend the stairs. This was the woman he wanted to spend the rest of his life with. He said nothing as he watched her.

When Ann reached the last step, Beecher stepped forward and took her hand. "You look beautiful this morning, but that is certainly no surprise to anyone," he said.

Ann smiled.

Beecher held out the small white box to her. "I brought you something," he said.

Ann took the box and said, "Thank you."

She opened the box and took out a white orchid corsage. Small strands of the white shreds cushioning the flower clung to it. "Oh, Beecher, it is beautiful. Thank you. Here, help me with my jacket and Mother can pin it on for me." Beecher carefully pulled the strands from the delicate flower before Ann handed it to her mother.

"Sure," said Beecher as he took the white pique jacket and held it for her to slip her arms in. When he slipped the jacket over her shoulders, he rested his hand on her back a second too long. The chill of his hand penetrated the jacket ever so slightly. Ann shivered and tuned away.

"Mother, please pin this gorgeous flower on my jacket," Ann said.

"Sure, dear. Beecher, this is such a lovely gesture. It was very sweet of you," said Mrs. White pointedly. She frowned at Ann.

Beecher watched Mrs. White pin the flower on Ann's jacket and waited. When she was done, he said, "Ready? I want to be there early enough for us to see the sun come up over the trees. I'm sure you will love it."

"Yes, I'm sure I will. I'm ready," she said, but she wasn't sure she was.

Beecher had the day planned out so that he could spend as much time as possible with Ann. They would attend the sunrise ceremony at Smith Lake then come back to town to church where he would sing a solo. He was sure Mrs. White would invite him to eat lunch with them then he would convince Ann to go for a ride back to the lake with him. There he had the real surprise waiting for her.

His plan was working.

Beecher parked the truck near the pavilion and got out. He walked around to the passenger door and straightened his tie. He wore a pink tie to match Ann's dress. His suit was brown like his eyes and the slowly rising sun struck his black hair as it filtered through the trees. He opened the door and took Ann's hand. This time she complied. She even smiled. She saw the sunlight hitting his hair.

Ann stepped out and gazed over the lake where the

sun was making its first red arch over the treetops. She smiled and said, "Oh, Beecher, it is beautiful!"

"I thought you would like it," he said.

Ann was mesmerized. She walked toward the pavilion and sat down on the back row. She smoothed her skirt and waited for Beecher to sit beside her.

Beecher put his arm around her and said, "Watch the lake right in front of those trees. See what the sunlight does to the water."

Suddenly it appeared as if a knife had sliced the water. A white streak like a silver sword split the lake in half. It only lasted a few seconds then the wind blew the trees so that their shadows covered the slice, but she had seen it.

Ann drew in her breath and said, "Oh my gosh, it is so beautiful!"

The wind was still quite chilled, so Ann shivered. Beecher felt her shudder, so he took his jacket off and draped it across her shoulders.

Ann protested, "No, Beecher. You'll be too cold."

Beecher smiled and said, "No, I'm fine. I won't let you freeze here in my domain."

Ann accepted this and continued to watch the sun rise. The choir had begun to sing, and their voices seemed to be one with the wind. She listened as the pastor delivered his sermon, but she kept her eyes on the water. She was overwhelmed with its beauty. Someone had set nearly fifty pots of Easter lilies near the shore, and they bled seamlessly into the floating water lilies in the shallow edge of the clear water. Just before the service ended a small fish jumped clear of the water and splashed, leaving glistening circles around him as he swam back to his friends. Three brown hawks circled above.

When they got back to Beecher's truck, Ann waited at the door for Beecher to open it. "Beecher, thank you for bringing me here. It is as beautiful as you promised. I see why you love it so much."

Beecher beamed. He had won. He would clinch the deal that afternoon. "Yes, I thought you would," he said. He wanted more than anything to kiss her as he stared into her face, but he didn't.

Ann watched Beecher during church. He stood beside her father with his deep baritone voice ringing clean and true. She couldn't help notice the physical similarities between him and her father. Both had dark hair and eyes and strong stocky builds. For a short second, Ann thought about what her children would look like if Beecher were their father.

Her next thoughts were of JT. She felt like she was cheating on him. He was so unlike Beecher she couldn't compare the two. JT, however, had abandoned her for his career. He had chosen to spend ten years, ten important years, in college, internship and residency. She couldn't understand why he didn't want her to be a part of those valuable years. If she married Beecher, she could have those ten years.

Just as Beecher had assumed, Mrs. White invited him to have dinner with them. He smiled and graciously accepted. This time he convinced Ann to ride with him to her home. Ann's mother had left most of her dinner in the oven when she left for church, so it took her only a few minutes to finish up and serve the meal. She had used

Ann's old Easter basket to hold sweet muffins and hot bread, and she insisted on telling Beecher how adorable Ann had been in her first Easter dress.

After dinner, out came the family albums and Beecher indulged Mrs. White lovingly as he allowed her to explain each picture to him. She sat beside him on the sofa with her skirt spread out beside her and turned the pages of the huge album laid open on the glass coffee table. A small bowl with Easter grass held wrapped chocolate eggs like the ones Ann had always gotten in her basket years earlier. Beecher unwrapped the pink and green tinsel on one of the eggs and took a bite while she talked.

Beecher laughed and nodded at all the correct times, so Mrs. White was sold. When the last page was turned and she shut the thick album, Beecher asked Mrs. White if he could borrow Ann for a couple of hours.

Mrs. White laughed and said, "Certainly, son."

Ann said, "Do I get a say in this?"

Beecher stood up quickly and said, "I'm sorry, Ann. Would you go for a ride with me? I have something I want to show you. It's a beautiful day, and I have a surprise for you."

Ann relaxed and replied, "Sure. Where are we going?"

"It is a secret. How else could it be a surprise. All I can say is, if I were you, I'd change clothes," said Beecher with a grin.

"And exactly what should I change into?" Ann asked.

"Jeans and boots would be a proper choice," Beecher said, still grinning.

FINDING ANN

Ann wrinkled her nose and looked askance at him.

"I promise it is safe," Beecher assured her.

Ann raised her eyebrows and questioned him, but she changed into jeans and boots, nevertheless.

While Ann was changing, Beecher whispered to Mrs. White, "I'd really like you and Mr. White to come with us. Would you consider following us in your car. I've bought some property to build a house on, and I'd like to show it to you, too. Your opinion is very important to me."

Mrs. White smiled and said, "We'll just be a minute." She left the room and motioned for her husband to follow her. Beecher looked about the room examining Ann's life in the furnishings of the room.

On each end of the crisp white mantle, sat a photo of Ann. One was of her riding a tricycle when she was probably five years old. The other was of her wearing a fitted pink and white satin and lace prom gown. Beecher guessed that was last year when she went to the prom with JT. He noted that the photo was of Ann only, not of Ann and JT. In the center of the mantle was a carving of a beaver, which Beecher thought odd. It appeared to have been hand carved from cedar. Lying in front of the beaver was a single dried rose with a faded ribbon tied around it. Before Beecher had time to hypothesize about its origin, Ann came back into the living room.

"Ok, here I am ready to go. So are you going to tell me where we are going?" Ann asked.

"Nope!" said Beecher.

They got into Beecher's truck then her parents backed their car out of the driveway, and he drove away with them following him. Mrs. White knew where they were going, so she smiled sweetly at Ann and waved out the window as Beecher's truck pulled away from her house.

"Close your eyes and keep them closed," said Beecher.

"You know I can't do that," said Ann.

"Sure you can. You are a talented girl," teased Beecher.

"We're going north—I can tell," said Ann.

"Maybe," said Beecher.

Ann giggled. "You are taking me back to Smith Lake, aren't you?" Ann asked.

"Maybe," said Beecher then he turned up the radio and began to sing along. Ann sighed and listened to his voice. She relaxed and began to hum along with him.

Beecher reached for her and said, "Come over here, gorgeous. I sing better with a beautiful girl on my arm."

Ann smiled and slid across the seat toward him. She sneaked a peek without his knowing she had opened her eyes. She closed them again. She knew they were going to Smith Lake, but she couldn't guess why.

When the truck finally pulled to a stop, Beecher said, "Ok, you can open your eyes now."

Ann looked around her and saw only trees. They were beautiful oak trees draped with moss. The land sloped gently down and appeared to be sandy. She wrinkled her eyebrows and asked, "Where are we? All I see is trees." Her parents pulled in behind them.

Mrs. White got out and looked around. Pretending not to know why they were there, she asked, "Beecher, this is a gorgeous spot, but why are we here?"

"Well," said Beecher, "You are looking at the site

of my new house. What do you think?"

"Really?" said Ann.

"Yes, ma'am. Follow me, and I'll show you the best part," Beecher said.

They walked along behind him as he held tree branches and brambles aside for them to pass. He stomped the underbrush down with his boots to make a path for them. The path led steadily down then suddenly they saw where he was taking them. The path opened up to a white sand beach bordering the crystal clear Smith Lake. They followed him down to the water's edge.

Mr. White said, "Well done, son. This is a perfect piece of land for a home."

Mrs. White looked at them both and said, "It is lovely, but don't you think it is too far out of town. It will take you forty-five minutes to get to work from here."

"Oh, that's alright with me. I like being out of town where it is quiet and I don't hear neighbors. We are building houses in this area anyway, so it won't be so far to work for me," replied Beecher.

"It really is beautiful, Beecher. It reminds me a little of our cabin down at Indian Pass. But I'm not sure I'd like living here all the time. Maybe for a vacation home, but not for all the time," Ann said.

Beecher smiled. He would convince her. He had time. "Well, maybe you will change your mind," he said.

It was clear to Ann now why this was so important to him. She backed away from him and stared at the lake. She stood like a statue, not knowing what to say or do.

Her father read her face and walked over to her. He put his arm around her and said, "Baby, why don't we go down to Indian Pass next weekend? Would you like that?"

Ann snuggled up to her father and smiled. "Yes, I'd like that very much," she said.

Her mother didn't like what she saw, but she didn't say anything. Mr. White held Ann close and turned her around then headed back up the hill. Beecher followed them without a word. He wasn't quite as sure now that he would win this war, let alone this particular battle. His feathers fell.

Mr. White took over, as was his practice. "Ann," he said when they got back to the car, "I've got something I want to get your opinion on at the cabin. What do you think about our taking a ride down to the coast now?"

"Sure, Daddy. I'd love to," Ann replied.

Mr. White turned to Mrs. White and said, "Cora, would you mind riding back to town with Beecher? Ann and I need a little father-daughter time."

Mrs. White raised her eyebrow and glared at him, but she acquiesced anyway. "Sure, if Beecher is a mind to be my chauffeur."

"Mrs. White, I'd be delighted!" Beecher said. He saw one more avenue to press his case. He knew Mrs. White was already on his side, and he'd make a brick wall out of that side.

Beecher took Mrs. White's hand and held the door for her. "Your chariot, my lady," he said.

Ann looked at him and rolled her eyes then got in the car with her father.

The trip to the coast took a little more than an hour and the conversation was serious.

"Daddy, I know Beecher is a nice guy, and I like

him, but I'm in love with JT," said Ann as soon as they pulled away from Smith Lake.

"I understand, Ann. Maybe you need to take a step back and give yourself some time," Mr. White said.

"JT will be home in another month, and maybe things will change. He pushed me away after Christmas, so I don't know if he loves me now. He's so focused on his career, he can't even see me now. I'm not sure he ever will again. I would wait forever for him if I thought he'd come back to me, but I'm not so sure he ever loved me anyway," Ann said.

"I don't have the answers, Ann, but don't be too hasty with your decision. Give your heart a chance to decide. JT is a fine young man. You should respect his dedication to his education," Mr. White said.

"I do respect his choice, Daddy, but I need to know he is dedicated to me also. I don't want to play second fiddle to his job or anything else. I want to be the most important thing in his life," Ann said.

Mr. White stared at the road ahead and grappled for the right words. He knew which she should choose, but he didn't know what to tell her at that moment to open her eyes. Something about Beecher seemed ominous to him, but he couldn't put his finger on it. This was his only child riding beside him. Her future was all that mattered to him.

When they got to the cabin at Indian Pass, he got out of the car and stood looking at the cabin and thinking of the first time he brought Ann there. He breathed deeply and said, "Come on inside, Ann. I want to talk to you."

Ann looked at him with tears in her eyes. She didn't know why, but she felt deep sadness. "Sure, Daddy," she said.

Mr. White unlocked the door and walked straight through to the back porch. He pulled two rocking chairs up side by side and said, "Sit with me, baby girl."

Ann looked at him strangely and did as she was told. She rarely saw him in this mood. She was suddenly frightened. She wondered if he was sick or maybe he had other bad news for her. Neither was true.

"Ann," he said, "I know you are at a crossroads, and I don't want to make this decision for you, but I want you to tread carefully. This will be the most important decision of your life. I can't make it for you, but I can tell you that I will always be behind you. I'm going to leave this cabin and some money to you exclusively, and I want you to promise me that you will never, no matter what, allow anyone else to hold title to this property. It is intended always to be your safety net. At some point, I'm going to put a substantial sum of cash here in a secure location that only you will know. If there is ever a time you need it, it is yours. You don't need to tell me or anyone else if you need the money. No one will know about it except you and me. Do you understand me?"

Ann's eyes widened. She looked into his face and saw fear. "Daddy, what are you saying? Do you know something I don't know?"

Mr. White laughed and said, "Yes, I know about life. It is a strange thing, you know. You are my baby girl, and nothing on this earth is more important than you are. I know about life's twists and turns. That's all. I want to make sure you are shielded from the foes I know about and some I don't."

"Who are the foes?" Ann asked. Now she was gripped by fear.

Mr. White took her hand and said, "I don't know, baby girl. I don't know. If I did, I would shoot them today."

That was the end of their conversation but not of their thoughts.

The next day, Ann received a letter from JT. He would be home in the middle of May. He said he missed her. The prom was two weeks away and Ann still had not made plans. She held out hope that he would come home, but her heart knew he wasn't going to be there.

Beecher was aware of this situation, so he hoped she would ask him to take her, but she didn't. Even with her mother's urging, she staunchly refused to attend her senior prom. She sat home alone that night. Beecher had asked to take her to a movie, but she told him she didn't feel well. She didn't.

JT arrived at her doorstep as promised on the nineteenth of May. Ann met him at the door. He was different. His hair was combed to the same side, his clothes were the same ones he wore on their last date, but he was different. So was Ann.

Ann smiled politely when she opened the door. "JT, come in. I'm so happy to see you. How are you?" she asked.

JT stepped inside and didn't know what to do. He thought he'd pick her up and swing her around and kiss her, but somehow that didn't seem appropriate this time. He was older and far more serious than the boy who had left her last fall. He bent down and kissed her gently on the forehead. When he did, he stood up and closed his eyes. He breathed deeply and said, "Oh, God, I forgot how good you smell." He couldn't help himself. He picked her up and squeezed her then kissed her.

Her face broke into a big grin. She kissed him as a woman kisses a man she loves.

"Oh, Ann, I've missed you so much. You are the last thing on my mind before I go to sleep and the first thing I see when I wake up," JT said.

"What?...I'm not in your dreams?" Ann replied, pretending to be astonished.

JT swung her around again and said, "Of course, you are! You are my dream girl—my only girl!"

Ann snuggled into his chest and was happy. The clouds went away.

It was Saturday. Ann and JT had the entire day together, so she asked him if he would take her down to the coast. He was happy to comply.

The morning was clear and bright. The sun bounced off the highway ahead of them, and they talked of carousels and Ferris wheels. They turned onto Oyster Shell Lane at 11:00am. It was the first time JT had been to the cabin.

When he pulled up in front of the cabin, JT's face softened. He said, almost in a whisper, "Ann it is magical. This must be the enchanted forest." And he smiled at her.

"Yes, it is," she replied. "Come inside with me."

They got out of the car and walked up onto the front porch. Ann unlocked the door and they went inside. Neither of them said anything. Ann took JT's hand and walked out to the back porch. The noon sun was making diamonds on the dark, brackish water behind the cabin. JT looked at Ann then back at the water. He smelled green smells all around him. Life was in the air. He sat down in one of the rocking chairs and patted his knee for Ann to sit. She did.

Ann wrapped her arms around his neck, and he began to rock. The property was shaded by spreading oaks trees, and a soft wind blew through from the Gulf on the other side of the road to the bayou in front of them. JT rocked and Ann felt herself go limp against his chest. She turned her face to his and kissed him softly at first.

JT's worries flew into the trees with the next breeze. He kissed her as he never had before. He was a boy when he left her. Now was a man holding the woman he loved. Ann smiled at him and stood up. She took his hand and led him into the bedroom. "Wait," she said. She walked over to the window and raised it half way. The wind began to feather across the down comforter on the bed. The smell of life from the salty bayou came into the cabin.

Ann walked back over to JT and slowly took off her shoes and folded back the covers of the bed while JT watched with a grin. He walked up to her and started unbuttoning her blouse. He gently folded it back from her shoulders and put his hand on her neck then slid it down to her chest. He reached around and unfastened her bra. It fell away and he held her against him as she lay down. He knelt on the floor beside the bed, no longer able to stand. He closed his eyes and felt her soft curves under his loving hand. He slowly, with her help, removed the rest of her clothes. Then he stood up and took off his clothes and lay down beside her.

JT looked at her smiling face and asked, "Are you sure?"

"Yes," she answered quietly.

He began to kiss her naked body as the soft breeze blew through the window and across their bodies. He knew better, but he was no longer in control of their journey. She had ruled his heart since the first day he saw her. Now she ruled his body as well.

The sun had begun to set when he came to his senses. He lay there beside her with his arms behind his head. He stared at the ceiling and wondered what he had done. He knew he had made a mistake, and he knew he was to blame. The only thing he didn't know was what to do now.

Finally he said, "Ann, I'm sorry."

Ann was almost asleep when his voice roused her. She caressed his face and looked into his eyes. "Why?" she asked.

"You know I love you, but we shouldn't have done that. I wasn't being fair to you. I wanted you so much, but I should have thought of your best interests and not my own. I'm sorry," he repeated.

Ann clutched the warm sheet beneath her body and wrapped it around her. She started to cry.

JT instinctively reached to comfort her, but she pushed him away. He got up and put his clothes on. He stood looking down at her for a frozen five minutes then walked out onto the back porch. He was rocking silently and watching the sun set the bayou on fire when she walked out and sat down beside him.

"Why?" she asked again.

"Why did we make love, or why am I sorry?" JT asked.

"Both, I guess," Ann replied.

The man in him wanted to say, "Damn it! We made love because I am a man and I'm in love with you," but instead, he said softly, "We made love because I love you, and I think you love me, but you are so young, and I should have known better. I can't marry you for a long time, and it isn't fair for me to hold your heart while you wait for me."

Ann had no idea how to answer him. She was confused and afraid. She took his hand and kissed it tenderly. The sun settled in the west as they held hands and hearts in the enchanted forest while the magic drifted away with the night fog and sank into the dark water.

On the ride home, they talked once again of carousels and Ferris wheels, but not of beds or bayous.

The next morning, JT sat beside Ann at church. Beecher sang a solo and never took his eyes off Ann. After church, Ann walked out to meet her parents holding JT's hand. Beecher nodded when he passed her but kept walking. He drove away in his red truck without looking back.

A galactic distance now separated JT and Ann. The gap seemed impossible to bridge and even more impossible to ignore.

JT called every day, but each day Ann made an excuse not to see him. When the weekend came, Ann said she didn't feel well, so she stayed home by herself on Saturday night. She had not heard from Beecher at all, and JT stopped calling. When the church bells rang the next day, JT was not there. This fact was not lost on Beecher as he looked down from the choir loft when services began. He smiled.

Beecher walked out with Ann's parents and smiled to see her waiting—alone. "Hi, Ann. You look beautiful as usual," he said.

"Thank you," Ann said with a sterile smile.

"Your mom said you weren't feeling well. I hope you are better now," Beecher said.

"Yes, thank you," said Ann.

Ann looked at her father, and he put his arm around her. Mrs. White gave him *the look*, and he smiled and said, "Let's go eat lunch, baby girl!" With that, he whisked his daughter away to the safety of his car, leaving Mrs. White with her mouth open. She rolled her eyes and smiled awkwardly at Beecher then followed father and daughter.

Cora White got into the car without a word, and the car rolled away. No one spoke on the way home, but Ann knew her father would get a tongue lashing. She also understood that his response would be a smile and "Yes, dear." But he would do it again, and all of them knew it. When it came to Ann, no one could stop him. He was her anchor—she was his treasure.

She caught him in his study later that evening. "Daddy, when did you know you were in love with Mother?" Ann asked.

"The first time I laid eyes on her, my dear," he replied.

"And did she love you from the first?" Ann asked.

"Well, not really. It took a little convincing," he answered.

Ann laughed. "I think JT and I both felt it when we met, but now I think maybe he has changed his mind," Ann said.

"What makes you think that?" Mr. White asked.

"It's complicated," Ann replied.

"Well, try me. I'm a reasonably intelligent fellow—I must be to have a daughter like you," Mr. White answered.

"Oh, I don't know. He is so focused on his career, I think he's sorry he's involved with me. I think he wants to break up with me," Ann explained, looking at the floor. She had never been good at lying to her father.

"It's more than that, isn't it, Ann?" Mr. White asked.

Ann closed her eyes and answered, "Yes."

"Do you want to tell me about it?" Mr. White asked.

Ann sighed and sat down. She frowned and answered, "I don't know."

"Ann, your heart has the answer. Why don't you go to see JT. Talk to him. I think he is probably as confused as you are. The only way to fix this is to talk about it. That's the way life is: problems never get better if you keep them bundled up inside your heart," Mr. White advised.

"So that's your advice—go talk to him?" asked Ann.

"If you love him, it is," Mr. White replied.

Ann looked down at the floor and asked, "Daddy, how did you feel the first time you made love to Mother?"

Mr. White raised his eyebrows and stumbled for a moment, "Happier than I've ever been in my life. Baby, that is the most sacred connection two people who love each other can have. If you are in love, that is the natural thing to do, and you will never be the same again once that happens."

Ann kept staring at the floor and didn't answer him, so he asked in a whisper, "Is that what this is about?"

Ann started to cry. "I love him, Daddy. I do."

Mr. White sat down beside Ann and put his arm around her. "Go to see him, baby. Talk to him."

When she had cried herself out, she picked up the phone and called JT. He was at her house ten minutes later to pick her up. They headed for the coast.

When they reached the cabin, JT stopped the car and looked at Ann. "Ann, let's go sit on the back porch and talk. I need you to understand my reaction. I love you more than life, and my love makes me want to protect you, never to harm you," he said.

She looked at him with tears in her eyes and answered, "I know."

They walked through the cabin and sat down in the rocking chairs once again, but there was no lightness in their steps.

JT held Ann's hand and stared out into the dark water. He couldn't look at Ann. "Ann, I do love you, but this is not the right time. I'm sorry I rushed you. That was not fair. We will have to live in separate worlds for the next few years, and I refuse to ask you not to have a life, to sit in your room and wait while I chase my dreams. You know you are the love of my life, but I want us to have a life as full and happy as we can. We can't do that right now. I want you with my whole body and soul, but that isn't fair to you," he said.

Ann jerked her hand away from his and stood up. She walked to the corner of the porch and looked out to the brighter part of the water where the bayou fed into the bay and its color went from black to sparkling diamonds of reflected sunlight. Finally she turned around and faced JT. He was still staring at the dark water in front of the cabin. "Look at me, JT! Don't I get any say in this? I am the one being hurt," she said.

JT was still rocking. He looked up at her and asked, "Is that what you really think? *You* are the one being hurt?"

"Yes, I do," Ann replied.

JT leaned his head back and closed his eyes. "You don't have a clue what is going on, do you?"

"Yes, I do. You made love to me then broke up with me! That's what is going on," Ann said.

"Oh, baby, come here," said JT.

JT stood up and Ann walked toward him. When he put his arms around her, she almost sank to the floor. JT scooped her up in his arms and carried her into the bedroom. He laid her down gently on the bed then lay down beside her. She turned away from him, and he wrapped her in his arms and held her. He could feel her crying. He wiped the tears from her eyes and kissed the back of her neck softly.

Finally Ann whispered, "Make love to me, JT."

"No, I won't take advantage of you, Ann. I love you, and right now loving you means letting you go," JT said softly.

Ann lay there for a while, slowly allowing his words into her brain. When her body finally stopped shaking, she said, "Okay, let's go home now. I understand." But she didn't.

Ann continued to go out with JT on the weekends during the summer, but it was never the same after that.

She knew the relationship was going nowhere, so by the time he left for college at the end of the summer, Ann was ready to get on with her life. Beecher was waiting.

Ann decided to put off her decision about college and work in her father's office until she was more certain of what she wanted to do with her life. She had graduated with honors and could have joined JT at the University of Florida, but she thought that might be a mistake. The dew was gone from the rose. Instead, she stumbled through life trying to force fate to make a decision for her. It did. Ann was unable to make a decision, so life stepped in and made it for her. JT washed away with the tide without even trying to swim against it.

5
MRS. BECKHAM

JT came by to see Ann as he was leaving town. She kissed him and waved to him as he drove away, but it wasn't nearly as painful as she had thought it might be. As soon as she closed the door, she heard the phone ringing.

"Ann, this is Beecher," he said.

"Hi, Beecher. How are you?" Ann asked. She had seen him in passing every Sunday, but she assumed he had lost interest in her. He smiled politely but had not asked her out.

"I'm fine. I was wondering if you'd like to go for a ride with me and maybe get some ice cream," Beecher said.

"Sure! When?" Ann asked.

"Well….what are you doing right now?" Beecher asked.

"Absolutely nothing," replied Ann.

In ten minutes, Beecher was standing at her door.

Ann answered the door to see a smiling Beecher Beckham. Before she could speak, a voice behind her said,

"Beecher! What a nice surprise. Come in!" It was Mrs. White.

"Thank you, Mrs. White. I'd like to take Ann out for ice cream, but, of course, we'd love for you to come along, too," Beecher said.

Mrs. White smiled broadly and replied, "What a sweet offer, but I'll let you two kids go and enjoy your time."

Ann rolled her eyes and said, "Let's go, Beecher."

The red truck parked at the Dairy Queen and Beecher went to the window and ordered two strawberry sundaes with whipped cream and a cherry. He brought the sundaes to the table under the wide oak tree where Ann was sitting. She giggled and said, "My favorite. I love strawberry sundaes!"

"I guessed it. So how have you been? It seems like years since I saw you," Beecher said.

"Beecher, you see me every Sunday. It's hardly been years since you saw me," Ann said.

Beecher laughed and sat down beside her, close to her. "Well, I meant *seeing you*, not just seeing you. You were occupied. I didn't want to intrude."

"It would hardly have been intruding. There was nothing there to intrude on," Ann said pointedly.

"Oh, I see," said Beecher. "So how about going out with me Friday night?" he asked.

"Sure, why not?" Ann replied.

"OK, I'll pick you up at 7:00. Would you like to go to the movies?" he asked.

"Sure, that sounds good to me," Ann answered.

Friday night came and Ann was happy to see

Beecher when he knocked on the door. She picked up her purse and scuttled out the door before her mother could come into the room.

Beecher noted that Ann was particularly chatty and made no attempt to push his hand away when he reached for her. He put his arm around her during the movie, and she snuggled close to him. When he brought her home after the movie, she asked him to sit on the porch steps and talk before he went home.

"Beecher, tell me what you are building now. Are you still building houses at Smith Lake?" she asked.

"Sure am. We've actually got three houses going now, big ones," he answered.

"Wow, you are a busy guy these days," Ann commented.

"Yes, that's how it works: I work, I make money, I build my own house. That's the plan. I work as many hours as I can because the more I work, the sooner I'll be able to build my own house," Beecher answered.

"You are an ambitious guy. How long do you think it will be before you can build your own house?" Ann asked.

"I plan to start by Christmas. I've managed to pay off the land, so it is free and clear for me to build. I'll build it slowly as I can pay for the materials myself," said Beecher.

"Wow! You mean you will have your own home? That's really cool. You still live with your parents now don't you?" Ann asked.

"No, Buddy and I got an apartment at the beginning of the summer. It is small, but we like it. He's not there much, so it works out just fine. I'll take you to see it if you want me to," Beecher said.

"I thought you would live at home to save for your house," Ann said.

"Well, everyone doesn't have Ward and June Cleaver for parents, Ann. My parents don't get along well, and I'd rather not be there. My dad sometimes isn't the nice guy he claims to be. He's got a temper, and he's pretty demanding about the way he wants things to be," Beecher said. He picked a leaf from the bush beside the steps and began to twist it in his hands.

Ann didn't say anything for a few minutes. She measured her thoughts carefully then said, "Beecher, I'm sorry. I didn't know. I suppose that is why you like being around my family so much. My mother adores you."

"Yes, I always like being in your house. Your family is all the things mine isn't. That's the kind of family I want to have someday. That's why I'm building my house. I want to settle down and have a family of my own," Beecher said.

"Me too," said Ann.

Beecher reached over and took her hand in his then brought it to his lips and kissed it. Ann looked into his eyes. She saw what she wanted to see.

Beecher kissed her gently at first then with all the passion she had been missing. His hands moved smoothly from her face to her body, but this time she didn't push him away.

Beecher became a regular visitor at Ann's house, and her mother doted on him. The whole family looked forward to Sunday mornings when Beecher stood beside

Ann's father and sang then they all came to Ann's house for lunch.

Halloween came and Beecher sat beside Ann handing out candy to gaily costumed children. Mrs. White had set up a sheet-ghost hanging from the porch ceiling and Beecher crouched behind the sheet and shook it when children started up the steps. When he jumped out and shouted "Boo!" they all screeched then laughed.

Ann watched Beecher play with the children and tease them. She began to think what a wonderful father he would become.

When all the children had left, Ann and Beecher remained on the porch looking out at the bright, full moon. Beecher held her hand and started to sing softly to her the lyrics of his favorite song, "The First Time Ever I Saw Your Face."

Ann was in a trance, enjoying the mood and Beecher's deep, mellow voice, but when he got to the line referring to the first time ever he lay with her, she sat up and said, "No, Beecher." Then she stood up to go inside.

Beecher grabbed her hand and said, "No, don't go in, Ann. It's just a song. I didn't write the lyrics, but you can't blame me for wanting you? Can you?"

Ann paused and looked down at him sitting in the swing. She stared at his hand holding hers then looked into his eyes. As was her habit now, she saw what she wanted to see and she heard what she wanted to hear. He read his lines well. "I'm sorry, Beecher. I'm tired. I need to go inside now. You need to go. This is going too fast for me," Ann said. She feared her own thoughts enough to pause, but that didn't last long.

Beecher left, but before he did, he kissed her tenderly. He held her neck softly with his hand and brought her face to his. When his lips finally left hers, he said, "We'll go as slow as you want to go, but I'll always be here." He smiled at her and walked down the steps. He got into his truck and didn't look back until he started to drive away. Ann was still standing with her hand on the door, but she was watching him. She had no idea how true it was when he said, "I'll always be here."

Ann stopped writing to JT after Halloween. When Thanksgiving came around, it was Beecher who sat at her table. Then came Christmas.

Ann walked out to the mail box to retrieve the day's accumulation of Christmas cards. She opened the box and pulled the stack out, sorting through them as she walked back up the sidewalk. She paused at the top of the steps and pulled out a bright red envelope. It had familiar writing on it. It was addressed to Miss Ann White. Another one just like it was addressed to Mr. and Mrs. Carl White.

The return address said only "JT." Ann ripped the envelope open and pulled out the card. It had a picture of a cheerful Santa on the front and the words "Merry Christmas" written in gold above Santa's cap. She quickly opened the card, expecting to find a message. She didn't. The printed card wished her a Merry Christmas, but there was no hand written message. The card was simply signed, "JT."

Ann stormed into the house and tossed the card into the trash before she went to her room and closed the door. She walked over to the window and pulled the curtain aside. She stood staring at the white picket fence across the street with tears streaming down her face. It would be nearly twenty years before she saw JT again.

The days crept toward the obvious conclusion, and Beecher became a fixture in her home. On Valentine's Day, her life changed forever.

Valentine's Day fell on Saturday that year, so Ann and Beecher made plans to go out to dinner and a movie. Ann bought a new red dress and matching heels. Beecher rang the doorbell promptly at 7:00. Mrs. White met him at the door and called out, "Ann, Sir Galahad is here."

"Come in, Beecher. Ann will be out in a minute. You know she has to make a grand entrance," Mrs. White said.

Mr. White frowned at her. "Now, Cora, that's not fair," he said.

"You know I'm kidding," Mrs. White said.

Beecher spoke up and smoothed the moment saying, "Every entrance Ann makes is grand to me. She's the most beautiful girl in the world."

Mr. White replied, "I agree, Beecher!"

Mrs. White added, "Of course, she is!" as Ann walked into the room.

"Wow!" said Beecher. "I thought you couldn't get any more gorgeous, but you did! Your chariot awaits, Cinderella. Hold onto your slippers."

"Thank you, Beecher. You look very handsome, yourself. Let's go," replied Ann.

Beecher held Ann's hand as she stepped up into the truck. He looked at her again and shook his head then closed the door with a big grin. They drove to a small café on the edge of town where Beecher had made reservations.

When the waiter seated them, he winked at Beecher. Ann raised her eyebrows and asked, "What is going on? That waiter just winked at you."

Beecher laughed and said, "Yes, he thinks I'm cute."

"Beecher, what are you up to this time?" Ann asked.

"It's a surprise," answered Beecher.

Ann looked askance at him and said, "I don't like surprises."

Beecher smiled his crooked Elvis smile and said, "You'll like this one." Then he turned his attention to the menu.

Ann picked up her menu as well. Beecher ordered their dinners, and all was going smoothly until they got ready for dessert. Beecher called the waiter over and said, "Josh, the lady would like one of your special desserts. Can you manage that?"

The waiter looked at Ann and winked again. He nodded and walked back into the kitchen. He came out a few minutes later with a dessert plate with a silver cover. He set the plate down in front of Beecher and said, "Perhaps you would like to serve it to the lady, Mr. Beckham."

Beecher said, "Thank you, Josh. Yes, I can take it from here."

Josh stepped back from the table but did not walk away. The room was full of ladies dressed in red and gentlemen catering to them on this sweethearts' day, but none looked as shocked as Ann when Beecher lifted the silver dome.

The silver plate with the dainty white lace doily held a stunning platinum band with a perfect emerald-cut diamond mounted on it. The light from candles placed around the room sparkled off the facets of the diamond.

Ann gasped and looked at Beecher. She appeared to be frightened of the ring. Beecher got up and took the ring from the plate. He kneeled in front of Ann and said, "Ann White, most beautiful girl in the world, will you marry me?"

Ann smiled and said, "Yes, I will!" When she held out her hand, Beecher slid the ring on the third finger of her left hand. The other diners had stopped to watch the show, and when she held up her hand to look at the ring, the room erupted with applause.

Ann didn't realize that JT's parents were among those diners.

The next day after church, Ann called Nell and told her she had something to show her. She said she would come by and pick Nell up and take her out for ice cream. Nell had a feeling she knew what Ann had to show her. Buddy had hinted that Beecher wanted to marry Ann, but she had hoped JT would come to his senses and intervene before that could happen.

When Ann drove up in Nell's driveway, Nell came out to the car and knew what had happened from the look on Ann's face. When Nell opened the door, Ann waved her hand in front of her.

"Oh, hell. Here we go. Ann you don't want to do that," Nell said.

"Nell! You are my best friend. You should be happy for me," Ann said.

"Yes, I am your best friend, but you aren't marrying the best man! It's that simple. If you tell me JT gave you that ring, I'll be happy," Nell said.

"You know that isn't the case, don't you, Nell?" asked a very disappointed Ann.

"Yes, I'm sure I know who gave you the ring," said Nell. She got in the car and sat down then she continued, "Ann, you know you are still in love with JT. You always will be."

"Nell, JT is not in love with me. That is a fact. How many times has he called me this year?" asked Ann, making a zero with her thumb and forefinger.

"And how many times have you tried to contact him?" asked Nell, making the same sign with her hand.

"Nell, what is it that you hate so much about Beecher?" asked Ann.

"He's an ass, Ann. You are just too blind to see it. Maybe you want to be blind. It's easier that way, isn't it?" asked Nell.

"Why do you say that, Nell? He's always very polite to you," said Ann.

"Forget it, Ann. You aren't going to listen to me anyway. I think I'll pass on the ice cream. Just take me home. I'll support whatever you think will make you happy," said Nell.

"So we are still friends, and you'll be my maid of honor? And you'll help me plan the wedding?" asked Ann.

"Sure. We've been friends almost our whole lives. I'll just be hoping I'm wrong about him. Buddy and I will get married sooner or later and we'll be a foursome anyway. Bring on the wedding cake and bridal showers.

You know I'll give you a shower, don't you?" asked Nell.

"I sure hope so. Nell, you'll love him when you get to know him. You have to admit, he is handsome," said Ann.

"He's not bad to look at, but I'm still worried. There is just something about him that I don't trust," said Nell.

The moment passed and Nell began to think maybe she was wrong. Ann was happier than she had seen her since she was with JT, and she admitted to herself that JT appeared to have dropped out of the picture. He was continuing down his path toward medical school and seldom came home. Nell's mother and JT's mother were close friends, so Nell occasionally got an update, but they didn't mention Ann. Nell rarely mentioned the updates to Ann and never to Buddy.

Spring flew by with Ann and Nell making plans for her big day in June. On June 22, Ann became Mrs. Beckham. Only once during the ceremony did Nell sense any hesitation in Ann's face, but only she noticed it. Buddy moved out of the apartment he shared with Beecher and Ann moved in.

Ann had managed to hold off Beecher's advances until the wedding night, but Beecher had no idea he was looking forward to that night far more than she. He never saw the tears streaming down her cheeks the first time he made love to her. He had conquered the maiden. He assumed she was merely modest and inexperienced.

After a short honeymoon trip to the beach, Ann began to organize her life as a housewife. She knew what she was supposed to do. Her mother had taught her well. She organized her dishes and pots and pans; she hung the towels embroidered with a silver "B"; she had dinner ready every day promptly at 6:00. She became Mrs. Beckham. From high school to housewife in the fell swoop of a rapid twelve months.

Beecher didn't want her to go to college. He assured her he could provide for her. He said they needed time to adjust to being husband and wife, so she stopped working for her father. After a while she stopped thinking about the future and just lived each day as it came.

By the end of September, she was pregnant. Beecher was elated, and Mrs. White was beside herself making baby clothes and planning a nursery. Beecher had begun building a home for them on his property at Smith Lake, but it would not be finished before the baby came, so Ann did the best she could to set up a nursery for the baby in their tiny apartment. She secretly hoped for a daughter, but Beecher refused to consider that possibility.

Mrs. White began to decorate and stock her guest bedroom as a nursery as soon as she got the news. She was in the nursery one day late in April when Ann arrived with a cardboard box full of diapers one of her friends had given her. When the nursery door opened, Mrs. White said, "Hello, Ann. I didn't expect you today."

Ann's body was round and heavy. She rubbed her expanding belly and replied, "I didn't plan to come, but Judy stopped by the apartment and left these diapers. She swears she's not having any more babies, so she insisted I take these. She says you can never have too many cloth diapers. Her last baby was allergic to the disposable ones, so she had stacks of these. I have nowhere to put them at the apartment."

"I saw Judy last week. She didn't look very happy. Is she okay?" Mrs. White asked.

"I think so. She's just not one of those girls cut out to be just a mother," Ann replied.

"Honey, all women are cut out to be mothers. That's part of natural biology. Some are, however, too selfish to fulfill their role," Mrs. White answered.

"Mother! All women are not alike," Ann insisted.

"Certainly, we are, dear. God made us to take care of men and raise our young. That is our God-given task, and we must follow our instructions. You've been reading too much of that new feminist propaganda," Mrs. White said. She picked up the stack of diapers and laid them on the changing table so she could refold them properly.

Ann rolled her eyes and said, "Mother, I am a person, not a pre-programmed robot."

"Yes, you are a person who is about to become a mother. I hope you see that as an occasion for joy," Mrs. White said without looking up from her task.

"Of course, I do, Mother! I am merely saying mothers are people. There is more to them than a person who changes diapers and cooks dinner," Ann said as she picked up the empty box that had held the diapers. "I'll put this in the trash on my way out," she added. She walked out of the nursery and quietly closed the door behind her.

Ann got into her car and stared at the street in front of her. She sat for several minutes before she pulled away from the curb. She knew her life was about to change, but she didn't think *she* was. Her mother had always taken care of her and her father. It had never crossed her mind to wonder who her mother really was. She was Mrs. White—

Ann's mother and Carl White's wife.

Cora White pulled the new white lace curtains back from the nursery window and watched her daughter. When Ann pulled away from the curb and started down the street, she let the lace fall back in place and went back to smoothing the sheets on the new crib mattress.

She had made the sheets to match the wallpaper she had hung so carefully on the walls, none of which her daughter seemed to notice. When she had finished in the room, she stood at the door admiring her work and wondering why her daughter had suddenly become someone she didn't know.

In June, John Bently Beckham arrived. He weighed eight pounds, twelve ounces and gave his mother considerable difficulty in delivery. Mrs. White insisted that Ann stay with her until she could recover. After all, she had completely outfitted a nursery for her first grandchild, and it was far more spacious than the small area Ann had managed to put together. She asked Beecher to come and stay with them as well, but he declined, saying he had to put in as many hours as possible to finish their new home so he could bring his little family to their real home.

Beecher knew he could not have sex with his wife for at least six weeks, so there really was no point in having her at home. Mrs. White was happy to help Ann with the midnight feedings of the baby. Beecher needed his sleep. By the time the house was finished, the baby should be sleeping all night, and Ann would be able to return to her role as Mrs. Beecher.

It was not until September that the new house was completed, but Beecher took much pride in bringing Ann and the baby up to see the progress each weekend. It was on one of these weekend visits that Ann began to see the other side of Beecher, the one that had caused her to shiver the first time she met him.

Ann had spread out a blanket on the floor of the unfinished kitchen and laid the sleepy baby down so that she could look at the rest of the house. Little John Bently fell asleep almost immediately, so Ann walked with Beecher back to the master bedroom. Ann was looking at paint samples Beecher had picked out when the baby screamed. They both ran back to the kitchen.

The baby was screaming uncontrollably when Ann picked him up. When she did, Beecher saw a fire ant crawling on his diaper. He flicked the ant off and stomped it on the floor. The red mark was already visible on the baby's leg where the ant had bitten him.

Beecher shouted, "You stupid bitch! You knew better than to lay him down on the floor. Why did I ever think you would be a good mother?"

Ann was stunned. She ran out the door carrying the crying baby. She walked down toward the water consoling the baby as she went. Beecher watched in disgust.

When she reached the water, Ann took a tissue from her pocket and wet it in the cold spring water then dabbed it on the ant bite. The baby's crying had changed to more of a whine as the sting abated. The cold water soothed the pain, and Ann hugged him to her chest. Her tears mixed with his.

Ann walked several hundred yards down the beach and tried to understand what had just happened. She wondered if she really was a bad mother as Beecher had said. She didn't even think about an insect biting the baby.

The house was nearly complete, and the doors had been closed and locked. It didn't occur to her that something could get in and harm her sleeping baby.

Clouds began to form behind the tree line so Ann started walking back toward the house, not knowing what she would do when she got there.

Ann was trembling when she walked back up the steps to the house. Beecher was standing on the porch glaring at her as she came up the steps.

"Do you realize you could have killed my son? He could be allergic to ant bites!" Beecher shouted at her.

"Beecher, you were standing there when I laid him down. Why didn't you tell me there were ants in the house?" Ann asked.

Beecher's hand came up before he could think. He slapped Ann across the face barely missing the baby then the baby began to scream again.

"See what you have done now. He's crying again!" Beecher shouted.

Ann ran through the house and out to the truck. She got in the truck and locked the doors, but she had no idea what she would do next. She looked around and saw that the keys were not in the truck. She had left her purse inside, so there was nothing she could do but sit and wait. After a few minutes in the summer heat, she had to roll the windows down. She didn't see Beecher anywhere, so all she could do was wait.

Finally she heard a car coming down the path. It was Buddy and Nell. Ann froze. She knew Nell would see the mark on her face. She opened her blouse and started feeding John Bently so neither of them would get in the

FINDING ANN

truck with her. She pulled her hair across her cheek and bent her head down as if she were looking at the baby.

When the car stopped beside her, Ann called out, "Beecher's inside. Go in and visit with him. I'll be in after I feed John Bently. He's always hungry."

They both waved and started inside. Ann sighed. She had bought a little time. She didn't hear any sounds inside the house, so after about thirty minutes, Ann got out of the truck and started inside. She held the baby against her face to hide the mark Beecher had left.

Beecher was standing in the kitchen when Ann walked up to the door. Beecher quickly opened the door and held it for her to come inside.

"Come in, honey. Did little John Bently get enough dinner? He's always hungry, you know," said Beecher as he lovingly put his hand on the baby's head.

"Yes, he's fine now," Ann said.

Nell said, "Oh, let me hold him. He's growing so fast I hardly recognize him." She put her arms up to take the baby, so Ann reluctantly let him go.

Nell took one look at her face and said, "Ann, come show me what you're going to do in John Bently's nursery."

"Sure," said Ann. When they got inside the baby's bedroom, Nell silently closed the door and whispered, "What the hell happened to your face?"

"Oh, nothing. A cabinet door had been left open, and I ran into it," replied Ann.

"Did the cabinet door have fingers?" asked Nell. Her scowl told Ann to tread lightly.

"Now Nell, don't get the wrong idea. Beecher

didn't mean to hurt me. It was an accident," Ann tried to explain.

"Accident, my ass! Slapping you in the face is no accident. You're coming with me. You will not live with that bastard another minute!" Nell whispered through clenched teeth. Nell had always been the one to stand up for herself and anyone else who needed it.

"Nell, I have a baby to raise. I cannot come with you. It won't happen again. I'm sure he won't do it again. He's been working so hard. He's just over tired. An ant bit the baby, and Beecher was upset then I argued with him. I shouldn't have done that," Ann explained.

"Ann, you are a fool. Men like that never change. Have you heard the stories about his mother? They would curl your hair. She had TB when Beecher was about 12 years old, so she went away to a TB sanatorium for a few months. When she came home, it wasn't more than a month until Beecher's father beat the shit out of her. That's why I didn't want you to marry him. He's got bad blood running through his veins. You have to get away from him!" Nell insisted.

They heard footsteps coming down the hall, so they both hushed. Beecher suddenly pushed the door open. He came into the room and said, "You ladies got this all figured out? Ann, I've got the color samples in the kitchen if you want to show them to Nell."

Nell gave Beecher what she called her "eat shit and die" look then Ann quickly took Beecher's arm and said, "Come on sweetheart, let's show them the master bedroom."

Beecher raised one eyebrow and returned Nell's

glare. The four of them walked down the hall to the master suite. Everyone could feel the ice in the room in the midst of August.

By the time Nell and Buddy got into their car, the handprint on Ann's face had almost disappeared, but Nell refused to leave until Ann and Beecher got into his truck and started driving away. Nell and Buddy left the property behind Ann and Beecher. As they were driving away, Ann pulled down the visor and watched the car behind her in the small vanity mirror on the visor. She could see Nell's animated face contorting and her hands gesturing as she told Buddy about what had happened to Ann.

Ann churned her thoughts as she wondered about Beecher's mother. She had always seemed to be a sweet lady. She was less than five feet tall and probably didn't weigh more than 100 pounds. Ann knew about her bout with TB, and she assumed that had left her weak. What she never guessed was the abuse she had suffered.

Beecher's father was tall and very muscular. Ann shivered as she considered what he could have done to his wife. Ann resolved that day never to allow her children to visit their home unattended. She was learning the lessons of life, one slap at a time. Her heart told her Beecher would never strike her again, but her head knew better.

Ann believed that John Bently needed a father, and she would endure whatever was necessary to make sure he had one.

Beecher sang along with the radio on the way home and chatted pleasantly with Ann about the finishing details of the house and a time schedule for their moving in. He told her he was spending his evenings organizing and packing up their possessions and that he would take care of everything for her. He assured her he would take very good care of her and his son.

"I will always make sure you and John Bently are provided for and protected. I know you are a little uneasy about living that far out of town, but you'll see—you will love it. We'll get John Bently a dog, and he can learn to fish and hunt right in his own front yard. I'll teach him to shoot as soon as he is old enough to hold a gun," Beecher told her.

"Beecher, I don't know about teaching him to fire a gun. Maybe that should wait until he is much older. I'm a little fearful of having all those guns around. Do you really need all of them?" Ann asked. Beecher already had his own collection of guns and was quite proud of them.

"You let me worry about that. You can raise our girls, but I'll raise my son the way I was raised," said Beecher.

Ann stared at the road ahead, but a cold shiver went down her spine. She thought to herself, "Oh no you won't!" But he did.

Beecher noted her silence and said, "Ann, you know I've built a secret room for my gun collection, and John Bently will not be able to get in there without me. I showed the room to Buddy today, but he'll be the only one besides me who can go in there. No one will even guess the room is there."

Ann looked at Beecher but didn't say anything. She was beginning to realize who he really was. "Why do you want so many guns, Beecher?"

"I'm going to protect what's mine. You don't

realize how many bad guys there are around us. Who knows, we may wind up in a civil war one day. The government is bound and determined to take our guns away so they can control us. By God, they'll never take my guns. I'll see to that. I've got enough ammo to hold them off for days. No sir! They'll never get me," he said.

Ann knew better than to reply. She looked at the telephone poles passing by in rhythmic order and she wondered. John Bently was sleeping peacefully when they arrived at Ann's parents' home. Beecher lovingly took the baby inside and kissed Ann's mother on the cheek.

"Take good care of my boy, Granny. I've got to go to work so I can finish the palace for my family. I'll see you all tomorrow," Beecher said as he dropped them off. He smiled and kissed Ann at the door then left.

He stopped in at the tavern between the White's house and his apartment. He stayed long enough and brought a friend home with him—no one saw him, and he smiled.

Nell was working two jobs, so Ann heard from her only once during the next few weeks. When she called, Ann cut her short and said she had to feed John Bently. Ann avoided conversation with her parents as well. She busied herself with making curtains and a new bedspread for her new home. Sewing allowed her to stay in her room and away from her parents, but this didn't go unnoticed by her father.

Mr. White came into Ann's room one afternoon and sat down on the bed behind her as she sat at the buzzing sewing machine. She didn't turn around, but continued to sew as her father sat behind her. "Ann, please stop for a minute and look at me," he said.

Ann stopped and turned around to face her father. "Sure, Daddy," she said.

"Ann, is everything ok with you and Beecher?" he asked.

"Yes, it's fine," Ann replied.

"Are you sure?" Mr. White asked again.

"Sure, Daddy. Why wouldn't it be?" Ann asked.

"Because I've known you nearly twenty years, and I see your face," Mr. White replied.

Ann took a deep breath and said, "Yes, Daddy, I'm fine. I'm just a little tired and ready to get into my own home."

"Ok, I'll have to trust you to tell me if you need me. You know you can call me any time, and I'll be there, don't you?" he continued. He raised his left eyebrow as he did when he was doubtful.

"Sure, Daddy. I'll remember that," Ann said. John Bently suddenly woke from his nap, and Ann rushed over to pick him up.

Mr. White watched her and knew she was hiding something from him, but he didn't know what it was. He sat on the edge of the bed rubbing his thumb across his chin. After that, Ann was more careful about hiding her emotions.

Moving day came in early December. Ann was thrilled with her new home even if she wasn't as pleased with its location. The house was situated on a high bluff overlooking the lake. The clear December sky warmed the landscape and set her world right. She loved being a mother and began to forget the earlier incident. Beecher was so proud of his home, he was happy for a while.

The trouble began when Ann was pregnant with her second child. John Bently was eighteen months old when Ann realized she was pregnant again. She was enjoying her role as wife and mother. True to his word, Beecher had not lost his temper with her again. Ann made sure everything in their lives went to his liking, so all was well.

Beecher provided well for them as he had said he would. He didn't allow her access to their bank account, but he gave her money whenever she asked. She had begun to relax. He loved his son, and he loved his wife. He protected them from the world.

Living at Smith Lake was not what she feared it to be. It was quiet and peaceful. She loved taking John Bently down to the shore to play in the water. She began teaching him to swim before he could walk. The water was cold and clear, and they all thrived in their new home.

Beecher had been adding to his gun collection on a regular basis, but as promised, he kept it locked. No one, not even Ann, saw what was inside. He made the money, so he got to say where it went. Ann had what she needed, so she never asked questions.

When Beecher first found out Ann was pregnant, he was ecstatic. He wanted little John Bently to have a brother. He said he wanted four sons to carry on his name and his business, which was fast becoming successful. He and Buddy were hiring more crews and building houses on their own now.

Beecher and Buddy came up with new names for the baby on a daily basis, but all of them were boys' names. Ann kept telling them that little girls were sweet too and that they had a 50/50 chance of needing a girl's name. Somehow this point was lost on the two men as they planned for teaching the boys to hunt and fish. Buddy and Nell had gotten married, but they still had no children, so Buddy was enjoying playing Daddy along with Beecher.

As Ann's pregnancy progressed, Beecher was more often late coming home. He told Ann he was working more hours to provide for his family. She believed him, but he often smelled of beer and cigarette smoke when he got home, and he didn't smoke, at least not that Ann knew about. But then there were a lot of things she didn't know at that point in her marriage.

In early August when Ann was one month away from her due date, Beecher came home late, as usual. He was particularly drunk that night. It was nearly midnight, and Ann was sleeping soundly when she heard Beecher fumbling with the door. She got up and came to the door to help him.

By the time Ann got to the door, Beecher was sitting on the floor of the porch. Ann opened the door and looked at the pitiful man slouching against the porch railing. How different this image was from the one she first saw of him. His physical looks had not changed so much, but her eyes saw him perhaps realistically for the first time.

She sighed and said, "Come on, Beecher. Let's get you inside."

Beecher raised his head and looked at his very pregnant wife and said, "Fuck you! I'm sleeping on my porch, and you can't stop me. You've fucked up everything else in my life—you can't fuck up my porch."

He had never spoken to Ann like this before. She

was suddenly frightened and felt more isolated than she had ever felt in her life. She froze for a few minutes then realized she had to try to get him inside. "Please, Beecher," she said, "Come inside."

Beecher made one feeble attempt to stand and grabbed Ann's leg. When he did, she went down. She had been standing at the top of the steps. She fell as if in slow motion down five steps and hit the concrete pad at the foot of the landing. She was knocked unconscious for a few minutes then came to with Beecher on his knees beside her.

"You fucked up again! Get up, woman!" he said.

Ann raised her head and looked into his face. She would never again see the man she married. She pushed herself up, one arm at a time. Off balance because of her advanced pregnancy, she wobbled and almost fell again, but she was able to hold onto the railing and get back up to the porch. She opened the door and went inside with Beecher gaping at her. She made her way to the bathroom where she glared at herself in the mirror. She saw a woman she didn't recognize. Her face was bloody, and purple bruises were already beginning to form on her arms.

How had she come to this juncture? She leaned against the vanity and cleaned her face as best she could then she got back into bed. She had no idea where Beecher was, but he was not in the room with her. She looked around the room then got up and locked the bedroom door. She was still awake when the sun began to rise over the trees. Every inch of her body hurt.

By 6:00 am her labor had started. She sat quietly thinking it was surely false labor and would abate, but it didn't. She had another month before the baby was due, but the pains kept coming and increasing in intensity. She heard Beecher drive away at 6:30, so she was alone.

She managed to get John Bently up and start feeding him, but every movement was a struggle. She finished feeding him then put him in his playpen. She sat down at the table with her head in her hands, wondering what to do.

She knew she could not drive herself to the hospital. Her parents were forty-five minutes away, so she waited still hoping labor would stop. By 10:00 am she knew that was not going to happen. John Bently was napping in his playpen, and she was sitting in the rocking chair when her water broke.

Ann called her doctor. The doctor told her to come to the hospital immediately, so she called her father.

"Daddy, my water broke. I have to go to the hospital. Can you come get me and take John Bently to Nell?" Ann said.

"Sure I can. Where's Beecher?" he said.

"I don't know. He left early this morning," Ann replied.

"Are you alright, baby," her father asked.

"Not really. I fell down the steps last night, and I think I hurt myself," Ann said.

"Why the hell didn't Beecher take you to the hospital last night?" Mr. White asked.

"I thought I was alright, Daddy. Just come get me—please," Ann said. The tone of her voice froze her father's heart.

"I'll be there as fast as I can. Call Amy Wilson, your neighbor. Ask her to stay with you until I get there.

Do you think you need an ambulance? I can't get there for at least 30 minutes," Mr. White said.

"No, I can wait for you. Just come now," Ann said.

"Okay, I'm leaving. I'm on your side of town, so I'll be there as fast as I can," he said.

Ann put the phone back in its cradle, but she didn't call anyone else. She didn't want anyone to see her. She wished her father didn't have to see her, but she had no choice. She dressed John Bently and packed a bag for him to stay with her mother then waited on the front porch. By the time her father got there, her pains were fifteen minutes apart.

When her father arrived, he was being escorted by a state trooper, who happened to be a family friend. He asked her a few questions then put her in his car. Mr. White put John Bently in his car, and they headed for the hospital. A State Trooper found Beecher at the Pine Tree Bar on Highway 20 and escorted him to the hospital as well. Mrs. White had called Nell, so when Ann arrived at the hospital, her family and best friend were gathered to wait. Nell took John Bently to the sitter Ann had used several times then returned to the hospital.

Only her father had seen Ann's face and bruised arms, and he chose not to tell them until after the baby arrived. Beecher had obviously been drinking, so it was a silent and mostly sullen group gathered around the delivery room door. Beecher had no idea how fortunate he was that none of them knew the truth.

They were there less than an hour when the nurse came out and told them little Kalee Jean had arrived. Nell jumped up and hugged the nurse then asked, "Can we see her now?"

The sweet-faced nurse said, "I'm afraid it will be a few minutes. We'll let you know."

Beecher was still sitting in his chair trying to smile. Mr. and Mrs. White were both standing in the hallway awaiting their first chance to see their new granddaughter. Only Beecher was still sitting. This fact was lost completely on Mrs. White. She chatted excitedly with the rest of the group then she looked at Beecher and said, "Beecher isn't this just the most wonderful thing? You have the best of both worlds now—a son and a daughter."

Beecher finally stood up and straightened his shoulders then said, "It sure is. I think Ann has known all along that it was a girl. She's had the name picked out for months. She wanted a girl."

"Well, didn't you?" a surprised Cora White asked.

"Oh, sure, but a boy would have been ok, too," he replied. He began to shift his weight from one foot to the other then said, "I'm going to have to get back to work. Tell Ann I'll be back soon. I just have to finish up some work."

Mr. White looked at him with that raised left eyebrow, and Beecher knew what he meant. They all stared at him as he left the room. He walked quickly down the hallway and disappeared around a clean white corner.

Nell was standing near Mr. White, so he heard her whisper, "Son of a bitch!"

He looked at her and smiled sadly. He nodded his head and whispered, "And you don't know the half of it. Wait until you see her."

Nell's eyes narrowed to brown slits and she said,

"Oh, tell me you are kidding!"

"Afraid not," said Mr. White.

Nell took a deep breath. She turned away toward the window and said, "I'll kill him!"

Mr. White walked up behind her and put his arm on her shoulder then said, "No, that's my job."

"Well then, I'll help. What are we going to do, Mr. White?" Nell asked.

"Do you know something I don't?" he asked.

"Not much. She won't talk to me. Do you know his father?" Nell asked.

"No," replied Mr. White.

"Well, let's just say the rotten apple doesn't fall far from the tree," replied Nell.

They were interrupted by the nurse who told them they could see the baby now, but Ann would be in recovery for a while. She assured them Ann was fine, but would not be out for a while. She gave them Ann's room number and said they could wait in the room.

All of them rushed down the hall to the nursery where little Kalee Jean was waiting. She was a tiny little thing, not like her big brother when he arrived. She had an oxygen mask on her face and was swaddled in a pink blanket. She was nearly bald and her eyes were closed, but they all declared her to be the most beautiful baby ever born. Noticeably missing was her father.

Little Kalee yawned and opened her eyes a bit to the delight of her audience. "Aww," said Nell. "I can't wait to hold her. She looks just like her mother—thank goodness."

"Yes, she does," said Mr. White. He smiled like only a grandfather can. For a split second, he forgot about her mother.

Finally they all walked down to Ann's room to wait. Mrs. White said, "I can't wait to get to my sewing machine. I want to make white eyelet and pink dotted swiss dresses. Sewing for a little boy just isn't as much fun as sewing for a girl. I'll embroider flowers and butterflies on everything. Oh, Carl, I don't think I was this excited even when Ann was born."

"No, I don't think you were. You are planning to stay with her for a while, aren't you?" he asked.

"Wild horses couldn't keep me away," she replied.

Mr. White looked at Nell and smiled. Both knew Beecher would be on his best behavior while the queen was watching. She was the only person completely fooled by Beecher's charm. He knew it was in his best interest to keep it that way.

They heard steps in the hallway and two nurses brought Ann into the room. They asked the family to step outside while they settled her into her bed. She smiled a dim smile as she was wheeled past them.

Nell's eyes widened and she sucked in her breath. She looked at Mr. White with frantic eyes. He nodded and said, "She fell down the front steps."

"Yes, and I'm Queen Elizabeth!" Nell replied.

"What was that, Nell?" Mrs. White asked.

"Nothing. I was wondering what happened to Ann's face," Nell said. She looked at Mr. White and waited.

"Ann said she fell down the front steps. That's what caused the early labor," Mr. White said as if he were reporting the weather.

"Oh, my! Why didn't she call us?" Mrs. White

asked.

"She must have thought she wasn't hurt," he replied.

"Well, is she?" Mrs. White asked.

"I guess we are about to find out," he said as the nurses opened the door.

Ann was still drowsy, but they bombarded her with questions as soon as they saw her face. Mrs. White asked, "Ann, what happened to you? Your face is a mess."

Ann turned away and covered her face with her hand. "Oh, it's nothing Mother. I fell down the front steps. Everything is fine now. Where is Beecher?" she asked.

Mrs. White answered before anyone else had a chance to, "He'll be right back, dear. He had some business to take care of."

Mr. White walked over to the window and looked down at the parking lot. He rested his hands on the windowsill and tried to remain calm. He would wait for everyone to leave. Then he would find out what really happened to his baby girl. Unfortunately, Ann never told him the truth, but he knew just as Nell did.

Beecher finally made it back to the hospital just before they brought Ann's dinner. He stopped by the nursery to look at his baby daughter through thick protective glass. The smells of a hospital made him nauseated, and they were all around him. He had spent too many hours in a hospital when he was a child. He was sober by then, so the reality of the night before began to penetrate his psyche.

Suddenly he remembered the day he turned twelve. It was the day his mother was checked into the TB sanatorium. He would spend the next few months with his father as his sole guardian. They visited his mother on the first day of every month for four months. He felt himself sitting outside the room while his father sat beside his mother's bed. He smelled ether and alcohol. He saw scrubbed white walls and dimly lit hallways. He heard patients coughing, and he saw a gurney wheeled down the hall with a body covered with a bleached white sheet. He waited for them to bring his mother out on her gurney. He wondered now if she might have wanted to take the ride on that gurney. He wondered how she felt the day they brought her home—and that day two weeks later.

Then an image of Ann flashed in front of him. He saw her falling, and falling. He heard her head hit the concrete. He started to cry.

A man walked up beside him and patted his shoulder. "I know how you feel, buddy. That's my daughter beside yours. The happiest day of my life—I swear it is. Sure brought tears to my eyes."

Beecher was jerked back into the moment. He replied, "Sure does."

He stood there mute until he could wipe the slate of his mind and gather his thoughts. He hurriedly walked back down to the florist shop on the ground floor and bought a dozen roses. When he got back up to Ann's room, she had little Kalee in her arms. He couldn't speak. He stood in the doorway and watched as his wife fed his child. She didn't hear him at first, but when she saw him she flinched and moved away from him.

"I'm so sorry," he said. He looked at her face and her arms and repeated, "I'm so sorry. I promise you, I'll never do that again. I was drunk. That wasn't me last night. That's not who I am. It will never happen again. Please forgive me," he said as he set the vase full of red roses on the table beside her bed. He put his hand on her arm and gently brushed across the bruises.

"Does it hurt?" he asked. She winced when he touched her.

"No, it doesn't hurt much. I'll be ok," she said as she turned her attention back to her daughter. "Do you want to hold her?" Ann asked.

"Will you let me hold her? I don't deserve to," Beecher admitted.

"Yes, you can hold her," Ann answered. She still had made no comment about his pleas, nor would she ever. There was no answer.

Beecher took his daughter in his arms and was still holding her when Mrs. White returned. "Awww...look at that—daddy and daughter bonding. How sweet," Mrs. White said. Mr. White came in behind her and walked around to the other side of Ann's bed.

"How are you, baby," he asked. He had yet to look at Beecher.

"I'm fine, Daddy. Thank you for coming to get me today," Ann said quietly.

"My pleasure. Every girl needs her daddy," he said. He finally looked at Beecher. The two locked eyes for a second too long. Each knew what the other was thinking.

Beecher handed the baby to Mrs. White who immediately began to make baby talk. She swayed back and forth with the baby in her arms and sang to her. "Ann, don't you think I should come stay with you for a while to help you? Two little ones is quite a lot to handle, you know," she said.

"Actually, Mother, I was thinking we might come stay with you like we did when John Bently was born. I think that would be better," Ann said.

"Sure. I would love that," said Mrs. White. She nudged Beecher's arm and said, "And, Daddy, you can come love your babies any time. We are always happy to see you."

Mr. White coughed and walked out into the hall. He walked down to the end of the hall and listened to the hushed voices talking in the rooms he passed. He was standing by the large window at the end of the hall when Nell came up the stairs.

"Oh, hello, Mr. White. Imagine finding you here. Visiting anyone in particular?" Nell asked.

"You might say that. Just the two prettiest girls in the world, who, I might add, have the prettiest friend in the world," said Mr. White. He put his arm around Nell as they walked down to Ann's room without saying anything.

Beecher had gone to get Ann a glass of juice when they got to the room. Mrs. White was still cooing over little Kalee.

"Well, well, well, Mrs. White, I know it was a struggle but you forced yourself to come up here to see this little princess. I can't imagine!" said Nell. "My turn," she added.

Mrs. White reluctantly handed the baby to Nell while Ann watched. Nell walked around to the back side of the bed and said, "Annie, you done yourself proud with this one! She's a keeper from what I see."

Ann laughed then stopped and rubbed her jaw. Mr. White watched.

Nell said, "Ann, what happened to your face?"

Ann tried to cover the bruises with her hand. "I tripped over a flower pot and fell down the stairs last night. You know how clumsy I am with this belly. I just didn't see the pot. I'm fine. It's nothing that won't heal," she said.

Nell looked at her eyes, but Ann would not meet her gaze. "Hmmm....looks like I need to take a baseball bat to that flower pot. I've got a nice, strong aluminum bat my brother used," Nell said.

Ann smiled a weak and unconvincing smile and replied, "Oh, I think Beecher will take care of it."

"But who's going to take care of Beecher?" Nell asked. She peered at Ann over the rims of her glasses.

Ann ignored her. Beecher walked back into the room, so the conversation died on the spot, but it was not finished. None of the banter was lost on Mr. White.

The next day Ann and little Kalee were released from the hospital, but as Ann had requested, they came to her parents' home rather than Beecher's.

Beecher was playing the adoring father, and Ann's parents were enjoying having Ann and her children in their home, but the following week brought another visitor. Captain Clenney of the Florida Highway Patrol paid a visit to his old friend, Carl White.

Clenney knocked on the door at 9:00 am Monday morning. Mrs. White answered the door. "Hello, Joe. It's nice to see you. We are so grateful for your helping Ann. I'm not sure she would have gotten to the hospital in time if you hadn't come to help her," said Ann's mother.

"Cora, you know I was happy to help. I thought I'd stop by and see how she and the baby are doing. Carl told me they were staying with you for a while. I think that was a wise decision," said Captain Clenney.

"Sure, let me see what she's doing now. I think she has both babies dressed and fed so she can relax and visit while I take over for a few minutes," said Mrs. White.

Ann heard their voices and came out carrying Kalee with John Bently following them.

Clenney saw them and said, "Well, hello, big fellow. I see you've got a pretty new sister. How do you like her?"

"She cry!" said John Bently.

Clenney laughed and said, "Well, that will get better. I promise."

John Bently ran to his grandmother and took her hand. "Granny, outside," he said, clutching her hand and pulling her toward the patio door.

"Sure! That's just what I had in mind. Let me get Kalee settled in her swing then you can run and play," said Mrs. White. Ann's father had gone all out for his new little family. He had bought a mechanical swing for Kalee and a small playground set for John Bently for the back yard. Kalee's swing was set up on the porch so they could all relax outside and watch the children.

When Mrs. White closed the door and was beyond hearing distance, Clenney asked, "Ann, is there anything you need to tell me?"

"Daddy sent you, didn't he?" Ann asked.

"He did mention it to me, but I would have come anyway. We always investigate when there is a situation like this. You'd be surprised how many women refuse to tell anyone when they are in danger. I don't want anything to happen to you. There are things you can do. You realize that don't you?" Clenney asked.

"There is nothing to tell. I fell. That's all," said Ann.

She got up and walked toward the porch. "I really need to go out with the children," she said as she paced back and forth.

"Ann, would you tell me exactly how the accident happened?" Clenney asked.

Ann stood with her back to him, pretending to watch the children. "I heard an owl outside, so I walked out onto the porch to listen to him. It was dark, so I didn't see the flower pot. That's all. I tripped," she said.

"And where was Beecher at the time?" Clenney asked.

"He wasn't home yet. He works late lots of nights. I got up and went inside. I thought I was okay until the next morning. That's when my labor started. It was early so I thought it was false labor and would stop. Beecher left early and went to work," Ann answered.

"Ann, he wasn't at work. We picked him up at the Pine Tree Bar and brought him to town. Buddy went back up there and got Beecher's truck. He was in no condition to drive. We didn't arrest him because he wasn't driving, but let me just say that we knew where to find him," Clenney said.

Ann turned around to face him with tears in her eyes. "I fell. Can you please let it go at that? Please let this go. I know you mean well, but this isn't making anything better," Ann said.

"Ann, I will go, but here's my card. I will always come if you call me. Beecher says he was there when you fell. I know you aren't telling me everything, but I can't force you to let me help you. Your father is worried about you, and so am I. We don't want you to have any more accidents. These things tend to get worse, not better," said Clenney.

"Thank you," said Ann. She walked over to the door and opened it for Clenney. "Don't worry, I'll be more careful next time," she added.

Clenney picked up his hat and put it on, but as he stepped out the door, he looked at Ann and said, "There had better not *be* any more *accidents*."

"There won't," said Ann before she closed the door. She leaned against the cold door and hung her head. At that point, she realized there would be more accidents, but she had two children. There was nothing she could do to change reality.

She was right about there being more accidents, but she was wrong about not being able to do anything about it. Unfortunately it took many years for her to figure that out. The accidents were few and far between, but that was only because Beecher found more excuses to be away from home, and Ann became a master at avoiding his triggers. She learned how to side step most of the time. She still believed that if she tried hard enough, he would be the husband she thought he would be. He chose his times and avoided hurting her in front of the children. Never did he abuse them as he did her.

6
WHERE IS ANN?

Ann couldn't identify when it happened, but it had. She had lost herself among the ruins of her marriage. She watched the clock, hearing every tick as the pendulum swung to and fro. It was a grandfather clock her parents had given her for her thirtieth birthday. She had loved the clock when she first saw it in her living room, but now it merely symbolized the ticking seconds until Beecher came home from work.

She was standing at the kitchen sink when she heard his truck inching down the path to the house. She looked at her hands holding the pink striped dish towel. The towel was trembling like the leaves on the trees outside her window. The wind blew quietly, with just enough force to make the leaves afraid.

Her children were away at college and wouldn't be home until Thanksgiving. Now the house was quiet, but when the screen door opened once more, she didn't know what would happen.

Beecher insisted he had seen a green sedan lurking behind the bushes by the gate. He said there was a man in the car looking at a photograph. He insisted the photograph was of Ann. She couldn't figure out why he thought that or how the man could have taken a photograph of her. She rarely left her house now, and then only with Beecher. He wanted to protect her from the strangers, especially the one in the green sedan.

Beecher asked her why she gave the man the photograph. She couldn't answer, so he slapped her—just once that time. He stormed out the door saying he would find out the truth no matter how hard she tried to hide it from him. She didn't know what she was hiding, but it didn't seem to matter anymore. Beecher built the truth of his own bricks and mortar just like he built houses, one lie at a time.

Ann had worked as Beecher's secretary and accountant for nearly twenty years, but he said she was flirting with the window salesman, so he forbade her to come to his office again. He also claimed she wasn't keeping the books accurately and was stealing his money a few dollars at a time. He calculated she had stolen $200,000 over the years, and he wanted to know what she had done with it. He suggested she had given it to the man with the photograph.

He had never paid her a salary, so he insisted she had taken the money to make up for it. He couldn't understand why she thought she needed money because he always gave her everything she wanted.

She recalled one particularly bitter argument over money. Ann went to a job site with Beecher on a cold winter morning, and while they sat in the car waiting for the sheetrock crew to show up, she asked why she had never received a pay check.

"Beecher," Ann said, "Why don't you want to pay me for my work? I do more work than two of your other employees."

"Sweetheart, I do pay you. Is there anything you want and don't have?" Beecher asked. "If there is, I'll buy it for you," he continued.

"No, but I just would like to have some money of my own. I don't even know how much money we have in the bank," Ann replied.

"Ann, we've been over this so many times. It is better if I handle the money. That isn't a woman's job. That is for a man to do. You don't need to worry. We have plenty of money," Beecher replied. "You need to read your Bible more. The Bible says, 'The husband is head of the wife as Christ is the head of the church, his body, of which he is the Savior. Now as the church submits to Christ, so also wives should submit to their husbands in everything: Ephesians 5:22-24'. It also says 'Wives, submit yourselves to your husbands, as is fitting in the Lord, Colossians: 3:18'. How can you argue with that? It is clear—I am doing what God wants me to do. I take care of you, and you obey me. Have you forgotten you promised on our wedding day that you would obey me?" asked Beecher.

Ann shuddered as she recalled that day. She believed at that point he actually thought he was doing the right thing. Somewhere between then and now, she had recognized the truth. She could no longer pretend not to see it. She couldn't identify when or how it happened, but it had happened. She had heard his father repeat the same verses and more.

Beecher's father had already become a tyrant by the time she met him, but it took Beecher ten years or more to get there. His journey from adoring husband to schizophrenic tyrant was a slow one, one with few definable steps, but it was as certain as the one he had watched his father travel. He had a model for his every move.

This thought hit Ann like ice water on a deep winter day. Had she managed to protect her son from this inheritance? She had covered up for Beecher for so many years, sometimes even she believed the lies she told herself. She wondered if John Bently believed them also. Beecher had been a strict father, but he had never abused his children as he did Ann. Had she played a part in Beecher's legacy? Did John Bently believe he should treat women like his father treated women? The horror of this thought made Ann physically ill.

Beecher saw to it that Ann had limited access to other people and ideas. Her children had not even had the benefit of seeing how Ann's parents treated each other in day-to-day life. Beecher had managed, without Ann's realizing it, to minimize their time with their grandparents. Ann never wanted them to spend time with his parents; therefore, they were not allowed to spend time with hers.

John Bently and Kalee had only Beecher and Ann for models. As she enabled Beecher, she disabled her children. She prayed for them to see life as it should be now that they were away at college. She feared it was too late.

Kalee was a quiet child who observed without comment. She had grown into a beautiful young woman, so when she wanted to go to college nearly a thousand miles from home, Ann was secretly very happy. This was one fight with Beecher that was worth the consequences. She had found a way to help Kalee escape. Ann wondered if her choice of college had anything to do with her father's behavior.

John Bently had chosen to go to the University of Central Florida. He came home often and spent most of his time with his father. Ann had no way of knowing how much damage had already been done, but she had no control over any of it. She wondered when she surrendered herself to the inevitable. Beecher washed over everyone in his path like a tsunami coming ashore in the middle of the silent night.

Beecher only allowed Ann to visit her parents when he could be with her. He told them Ann was a bad driver so he had to drive her to keep her safe. He thought her eyesight was failing. That must be why she didn't see the man with the photograph. He hired a private investigator to find out who the man in the green sedan was. He also wanted to know where Ann kept the $200,000 she had stolen from him. The investigator never found either the sedan or the money. He hired another one who turned out to be equally incompetent.

Life became a game of survival. Some days she wondered why she kept breathing. She didn't realize Ann had gone away with the man in the green sedan. She floated from room to room and back again, hiding, ducking the blows that came her way, anesthetized by life.

She was startled back from her surreal journey by the ringing phone. It was Nell.

"Ann, did you know about our class reunion?" Nell asked.

Ann had not talked to Nell in nearly a year, so she was shocked to hear her voice. "No, I didn't," Ann replied.

"I thought not. Ann, do you get all your mail?" Nell asked.

"Sure, I guess so. Beecher picks it up on the way into the property at night. He says there is someone stalking our property, so he doesn't want me walking out to the mail box," Ann replied.

Ann waited for a response. All she heard was a deep sigh and a long pause then Nell said quietly, "Oh, I see. Well, how about I bring you a copy of the invitation? If you want to go, you can go with Buddy and me. It would be good for you to get out. When was the last time you went out without Beecher?"

"I don't go out much anymore. I like staying home. I make quilts and paint a little. I suppose I've turned into an old stay-at-home," Ann said.

"Yes, I see that. I am not busy right now, so may I come up to visit with you and bring the invitation?" Nell asked.

"Sure. I'd love to see you," said Ann.

"Would you?" asked Nell.

"Of course, I would. I'm always happy to see you," Ann replied.

"When is Beecher coming home?" Nell asked.

"Not until after 6:00 tonight," Ann said.

"Fine, I'll be there in 45 minutes," said Nell.

"Wonderful! I'm looking forward to seeing you," said Ann.

Ann went into her bathroom and washed her face. She turned her face from side to side checking for marks. She picked up her makeup and dabbed concealing dots on three faint marks. They had been there a while, but she didn't want Nell to suspect problems.

Nell already hated Beecher, so no need to fan the fire. That would just cause more problems. The worst beating she had taken was after someone at church suggested to the minister that something was wrong with Ann. He called her into his study the following week and questioned her for an hour. Beecher happened to come by the church and see the car. That was all it took. Ann realized that if Beecher found out Nell was at their house, she would pay. It didn't much matter anymore what she did or didn't do. His mind created his own reality, and she paid for each misstep he created.

Ann patted her face with a pink power puff and smiled at the thought of seeing Nell again. She walked around the living room making certain everything was neat and tidy then she made a fresh pot of coffee and waited. Soon Nell's car pulled up behind the house. Ann saw her from the kitchen window and went out to greet her.

Summer was hanging on, but the leaves had begun to wither and vines were turning brown along the fence. Someone nearby was burning trash and a hint of smoke drifted by. They had been twenty years out of school, but Nell seemed to be the same girl she was then.

"Nell, I'm so happy to see you. Please come in," said Ann.

Nell hugged Ann and asked, "How are you?"

"Fine, I'm fine," Ann replied with her customary smile.

"No, I mean really how are you?" Nell repeated.

Ann backed away a bit and said, "Nell, really, I'm fine."

Nell took a deep breath and said, "Well, fine. Are you going to the reunion or not?"

"I don't know. When is it? Tell me about it," Ann said. "I'd like to see our old friends."

"All of our old friends?" Nell asked.

Ann laughed and answered, "Well, maybe not *all* our old friends. You don't think JT will be there do you?"

Nell looked at Ann very seriously and asked, "Would that be a problem?"

"Nell, you know it would," answered Ann.

"For you or for Beecher?" asked Nell.

"Both," replied Ann.

"Why for you?" asked Nell even though she knew the answer. She wanted to hear Ann say it.

"You can't figure that one out? You're a smart girl. Think about it," said Ann.

"I know the answer. Do you?" Nell said.

"Probably," replied Ann.

"I doubt that. Ann do you still love JT?" asked Nell.

Ann got up and walked around the kitchen bar. She stared at the cabinets for a long moment then picked up a coffee cup. "Let's have a cup of coffee, Nell," she said.

"Okay," said Nell. She sat down and waited.

Ann set two cups of coffee down on the counter then sat down beside Nell. "Nell, we've been friends nearly all our lives, and you know me maybe better than I know myself. I love you, but your answers are always flippant and defiant. Life just isn't that simple," Ann said.

"Yes, it is that simple. Ann, he hurts you, and he runs around on you. You know that. So does everyone else in town with the possible exception of your mother. What is it going to take to get you to leave him?" Nell asked.

Ann suddenly looked deeply into Nell's dark eyes. "Does he run around on me? Are you sure?" she asked.

"Of course, he does. Do you honestly doubt it?" Nell asked.

"Sometimes," said Ann.

"Ann, I've seen him walking down the street with a woman—in the middle of the day! She works at the bank. He doesn't even try to hide anymore. One of these days he's going to bring you a gift you can't get rid of. Some of the women he sees are not nice people, and he's not *nice people!*" said Nell.

Ann started to cry. Nell laid her hand on Ann's shoulder and realized how thin she had become. She wanted to get in her car and drive away to *fix* the problem—permanently, but she didn't. She said, "Ann, let me help you. You can come with me now."

Ann lifted her head and took a sip of her coffee. She set the cup down and wrapped both her hands around the cup as if to warm them. She looked at the rings on her finger and said, "Nell, I'm his wife. I'm the mother of two children. That is who I am. I don't know how to be anyone else. That is who I am. I am Beecher's wife: that is my identity. If I'm not Beecher's wife, I don't exist."

"Ann, have you lost your mind? You are Ann

White! That's who you are—not somebody's wife or somebody's daughter or mother! You are *Ann*," said Nell.

"Who is Ann White? She got lost long ago. She got lost the day she became Ann Beckham. Woman was created for man, not the other way around. The Bible tells us that. I am his woman. The Bible says, 'The husband is the head of the wife as Christ is the head of the church, his body, of which he is the Savior. Now as the church submits to Christ, so also wives should submit to their husbands in everything.' That is Ephesians 5:22-24. My mother gave me a framed copy of that when I got married. She hung it on the wall in my bedroom so I'd never forget it. She adores Beecher. How do you think she would feel if she knew my thoughts?" Ann said.

Nell threw her head back and said, "Shit!" She got up and walked over to the window. She stood there while Ann watched her in silence.

Finally she turned around and faced Ann. "Ann, that is a bucket of crap, and you know it. That is total bullshit! You need to pull your head out of your ass and look in the mirror. You are *ANN*! You don't belong to anyone! Please come with me now. You have no business staying in this house one more minute."

"Nell, you know I can't do that. Where would I live? I can't live with you. Beecher would kill you, and I'm not joking when I say that," Ann insisted.

"Bullshit! I'll never be afraid of that bastard. Let him try to come after me. Buddy will stop him in his tracks if he is lucky enough to get past me," Nell shouted.

"Nell, I would never put you in harm's way. Besides, my parents would disown me. How would I live?"

Ann asked.

"This is a community property state. The state would give you half of what you and Beecher have accumulated together. You could make him pay alimony," said Nell.

"The state can't give me half of something they don't know about. I have no idea how much money Beecher has," said Ann.

Nell stormed across the room to Ann and said, "Wait a minute…you mean you don't *know* how much money you have?"

"I don't have any money, and I don't know how much Beecher has. He takes care of the finances. I think he may be putting money in off-shore banks," said Ann.

"You have got to be kidding me! Why do you think that and where does he keep his investments that you know about?" asked Nell.

"I have no idea. That's the problem. I saw some mail once from a bank in the Bahamas and when I asked him about it, he got very angry. I don't ask any questions now," answered Ann. The weight of her plight began to sink in, so she sat down heavily on the sofa.

"How many years do you think I'd get for killing him?" asked Nell.

"Now Nell, you know you wouldn't do that," said Ann.

"The hell I wouldn't! I'd have no problem pulling that trigger," said Nell.

"Ann take your shirt off now!" said Nell.

Ann looked at her as if she had lost her mind. "Why?" she asked.

"Just do it," Nell said.

Ann unbuttoned her shirt and slid it off her shoulders. When her back was bare, Nell had her answer. Just below her shoulder blades were two bruises old enough to have become yellow blotches. "You weren't going to tell me about these bruises, were you?" Nell asked.

"No," said Ann.

"Why not?" asked Nell.

"Why?" replied Ann.

Nell closed her eyes and hung her head. She shook her head from side to side and asked quietly, "Oh, Ann, what are we going to do? Surely you don't think your parents expect you to take this abuse and stay with Beecher, do you?"

"Probably not. You don't understand, Nell. It really is complicated. My mother is so against divorce. I have no money and no way to support myself, my children would be devastated, I would be humiliated, and no one would believe me. The list goes on and on. I can't do it. It doesn't happen often. I am better off where I am and in a world I no longer belong to. I lost Ann a long time ago. She is not hiding, she is gone," replied Ann.

"No, she isn't gone. I see her in front of me. There isn't much I can do for you, but I can bring you back into the world. Why don't we start with the reunion? If Beecher refuses to go, you can go with Buddy and me, and if Buddy balks, you and I will go without them," Nell said. She raised her eyebrow and issued an unspoken dare to her best friend. Then she smiled.

"I don't think that is such a good idea, Nell. Beecher will be furious," Ann said.

"No, he won't. I'll convince Buddy to get him to go. He and Buddy have worked together a long time, so he knows Beecher, or he thinks he does. Believe me, at this point, he cares a lot more about you than he does about Beecher. He's seen Beecher show his ass enough times to know the score. He has to watch Beecher like a hawk to keep him from cheating him in business deals. I'll talk to Buddy. We'll make sure you get to go to the reunion, and we'll keep you safe," said Nell.

"I'd actually love to go—if I could without upsetting Beecher. I haven't seen any of my friends in so long. I'd love to know how some of them are," Ann said. She finally smiled and put her shirt back on. It felt good to know that Nell was finally aware of her situation. Being alone is sometimes worse than the abuse itself. In reality nothing had changed, but in her mind it had. Something about saying those things out loud made them real, and real demons are easier targets than those held only in one mind.

"Ann, you never answered my question about JT. Are you still in love with him?" Nell asked.

"It doesn't matter, Nell. He fell out of love with me years ago. My feelings are completely irrelevant," Ann answered.

"How do you know that?" asked Nell.

"Your memory must have failed you. He left me, remember that?" said Ann.

"Ann, he went off to college, not to the North Pole. He didn't leave you—he went to college. There is a difference. I want to know if you are still in love with him," asked Nell pointedly.

"What does it feel like to be in love? I don't

remember. That is something young people experience. I'm not young anymore," replied Ann.

"Do you ever dream about him?" asked Nell.

"I don't dream about anything anymore. There's no point in dreaming," said Ann.

Ann was standing at the end of the bar wiping the counter with a clean, white cloth. Nell looked at her and felt a pain she had never known before. She walked over to Ann whose motion seemed to be suspended in time above a stain on the counter that she couldn't remove. Nell put her arms around Ann, and Ann allowed Nell to enfold her for a moment in love.

Ann began to sob, quietly at first then with grief like Nell had never seen. Nell didn't say anything; she just held her friend until the sobs subsided.

The two friends sat in rocking chairs on the wide veranda overlooking Smith Lake and rocked. After a prolonged silence, Nell asked, "Ann, have you ever considered going back to school—maybe just taking a few classes at the community college? You could take up photography, or maybe find a career you would enjoy. It isn't good for you to stay here alone all the time."

"Beecher would never let me do that. He believes a woman's place is in the home," said Ann.

"Bullshit! A woman's place is where ever she wants to be. Do you want to be here alone all the time?" asked Nell.

"I don't know where I want to be," said Ann.

"Well, I'm guessing it isn't here. Why not consider my suggestion? I'll take the classes with you. What the hell? Why don't we take up painting and paint nude male portraits? That sounds like fun," suggested Nell.

Finally Ann laughed. "Maybe we could paint the man in the green sedan. That would be nice," said Ann.

"Whoa! Who is the man in the green sedan? You never told me about that," said Nell.

"It would be funny if it weren't so serious. Beecher thinks there is someone stalking us. He thinks the man might be my boyfriend. He says he's seen him several times outside the gate. He locks the gate every day when he leaves and checks to make sure I haven't unlocked it during the day. He says he wants to have surveillance cameras installed to protect me from this mysterious man," explained Ann.

"You must be kidding!" said Nell.

"I wish I were," said Ann. She sighed and shook her head. "He thinks the man wants me because of the $200,000 I have hidden."

"Holy crap! You have $200,000?" asked the stunned Nell.

Ann laughed and said, "I guess so. That's what Beecher says. He says I stole that from his business while I was working for him. Problem is, my memory fails me. I can't remember where it is. Trust me, he has tried to help me remember where I hid it."

"Does that crazy bastard realize if you had $200,000, you'd leave his sorry ass?" Nell asked. She got up and stood in front of Ann looking down at her in disbelief.

"Guess not. I think he's just like his father. He accuses Beecher's mom of all kinds of outrageous things that are obviously not true," explained Ann.

"You are saying he's crazy, as in certifiably mental?" asked Nell.

"That would be my guess," said Ann.

Nell sat back down and started rocking, trying to absorb what Ann had told her. Finally she said, "Oh my God, Ann, you are in a lot more trouble than I thought. Please come with me now."

"You know I can't," said Ann. They both bowed their heads and sighed.

A few words were exchanged after that, but mostly they rocked. Nell looked at her watch when the sun neared the tall pines on the far shore. It was 5:30, so she left her childhood friend and started making plans.

The reunion was being held at the Radisson Hotel. Nell made reservations for four for the reunion and reserved two rooms at the hotel for the night. Buddy convinced Beecher they could enjoy the night more if they didn't have to drive home. All was well. Buddy did his job. He reminded Beecher there would be lots of women there, all of them dressed up and looking fine. He didn't mention the fact that Ann would be dressed up as well. That never occurred to Beecher. Ann was Mrs. Beckham. She belonged to him.

7
THE REUNION

The reunion started out well enough. Ann and Nell walked over to the table at the entrance to the ballroom and signed in. They picked up name badges for themselves and their husbands. The badges had little photos of the class member taken from their senior portrait. They laughed at how much they had all changed. Betty Sue Anderson was handing out the badges. She joked with them as she searched for their names.

"I don't know about you two girls, but I don't think I'm any older. My mirror disagrees, but I still think I'm about to graduate," Betty Sue said. "Oh, here you are, Ann. Here's your badge and Nell, here's yours," she said.

"Thank you, Betty Sue. It's great to see you again," said Nell.

"Same here, Nell. You and Ann are still inseparable after all these years. I think that's great. My best friend died last year. Treasure your friendship. I had not seen Amy for many years when I got the word she had died," Betty Sue said.

"Oh, I'm so sorry," said Ann. "What happened to her?"

"I'm not really sure. Rumor has it that her husband shot her, but her mother says she committed suicide. I don't know. I wish I had kept in touch with her. We never know how we can change someone's life by simply being there. I'll always wonder if she would still be here if I had been a better friend," said Betty Sue.

Ann touched her hand and said, "Betty Sue, you can't always know when you are needed. I'm sure you were a good friend. I'm truly sorry for your loss," said Ann.

Ann looked at Nell and linked her arm with Nell's. They walked together over to their husbands and pinned their badges on their jackets.

The band was setting up on the stage and a long buffet table had been set up along one side of the room. The lights were dim and candles were glimmering on each table. Nell chose a table near the center of the room and put her purse down then said, "Ann, let's go get a plate and sit down to wait for more guests to get here before we start making the rounds. Buddy, you and Beecher get some drinks for us, and we'll bring you some food."

"Sounds good to me," said Buddy. "Come on Beecher. Let's hit the bar."

Beecher followed Buddy to the bar as he looked around the room. "Hey, Buddy, there's Sally McGinty. Remember her?" said Beecher.

Buddy laughed and asked, "Didn't you have the hots for her in the tenth grade?"

"Oh, man, did I ever. She's the first girl I ever

screwed. What a lay! Let's just say, she was *experienced*," said Beecher.

"Yeah, that's what I heard. What a way to break a young man in!" added Buddy.

"You got that right. I wonder if she's still puttin' out. I think I'll go say hello for old time's sake," said Beecher.

"Old times, my ass. Beecher, mind your manners. Your wife is here—remember that little detail?" said Buddy.

"So?" replied Beecher. "What difference does that make?"

"Beecher, can't you keep it in your pants just one night. Come on, man. Let's go sit down," said Buddy.

Beecher followed him to the table, but he kept his eyes on Sally. They sat down at the table before Ann and Nell returned. Buddy whispered to Beecher, "Beech, play it cool tonight. This is a special night for the girls. Let's make sure they have fun. This is not our night. We are married to two very special women. Let's make them feel special tonight."

Beecher looked at Buddy and sneered. He replied, "They have special husbands. That's what makes them special."

Buddy looked at him and said, "You know, Beecher, you really are an ass."

Beecher was still laughing when the girls got back to the table.

"What's so funny, guys?" Nell asked.

"Oh, nothing. We're just having a good time," Buddy said. He gave Beecher *the look* when he opened his mouth to speak, so he didn't.

Ruth Perkins came by the table and spotted Ann. "Ann! How wonderful to see you. You look great."

Ann got up and hugged Ruth. "You look wonderful too, Ruth. How have you been?" asked Ann.

"Great, Ann. I teach at the University. I love it. James and I live out near Lake Ella. We don't have any kids, just two ornery dogs and a prissy cat. That's all I can handle," replied Ruth. "How about you?"

"Oh, I'm great. I'm just a housewife, but I've got a couple of great kids," replied Ann.

"That's wonderful. I missed out on the kids part of life. That never seemed to fit into my schedule. Oh, look! There's Becky. Let me go say hello to her," said Ruth as she rushed off.

Nell had wandered off and was talking to several other classmates. Ann watched her and looked around the room. She saw several old friends, but waited for Nell to return before she left the table.

When Nell made her way back to the table, Ann joined her to make the rounds in the room and find as many old friends as she could. Ann was dressed in a deep blue turtleneck sweater and a matching long satin skirt with a slit on one side. Her hair was swept up in a French twist, which she had fastened with a sapphire clip on one side. The gray strands in her hair merely made her more interesting instead of aging her. She wore time well in spite of the unseen stress she had lived with for the past twenty years. She smiled at everyone she passed and chatted with special friends.

Then she saw him. She froze. "Nell," she said,

"Look over there. Look who is with Judy." Ann's face went pale and her breath stopped.

"Oh, shit! Here we go. I never dreamed he would show up for this. He doesn't date anyone, so I was sure he wouldn't come tonight. He wasn't in our class. I'm sorry, Ann. I thought you were safe," said Nell, stumbling to apologize to Ann. The napkin Nell had wrapped around her drink was dancing with her nervous hand.

"What do I do now?" Ann asked.

"What do you want to do?" Nell replied.

"You don't want to know," said Ann.

"Hells, bells, girl! Do it! You only live once. What can Beecher do here?" said Nell.

"I can't, Nell. I would pay more than it would be worth. Let's go back and sit down with the guys," Ann said, but it was too late. JT had seen them.

JT excused himself from the conversation he was having with several old friends and walked over to Ann before she could react. "Ann, how are you? I'm so happy to see you," he said.

Ann felt as if her heart would leap from her chest, but she managed to speak. Very softly she said, "I'm ok. It is wonderful to see you, too."

"Ann, you look so pretty tonight. It's as if no time has passed for you," said JT. He paused and stood looking down at her as if he were about to kiss her.

Ann looked up at him and wished he would, but they both knew that could not be. She felt as if she were being zapped by some invisible power source. She wanted to move, but she couldn't.

After the longest minute in her life, JT said, "Ann,

I'm sorry."

Ann raised her eyebrows and replied, "For what?"

JT's answer was thwarted by Nell's intrusion. "Hi, JT. We never expected to see you here," she said. She knew she had to break this up before Ann got hurt. Encouraging her was a whim, but now it was reality about to slap them in the face.

Brought back to the moment, JT replied, "No, I didn't expect to be here, but Judy works in my office, and she didn't want to come alone. She talked me into coming with her. She's only been divorced a few months, and I thought she needed this, so I agreed. I don't go out much, so who knows? Maybe she took pity on me. She's the best nurse I ever worked with, so I need to keep her happy. She's so good with the kids; she makes them feel comfortable with uncomfortable procedures. She's a treasure."

Ann watched his mouth without hearing a word he said. She was entranced, but she managed to smile. She felt as if she were in a barrel with voices echoing around her, but she couldn't see any of the people.

Nell replied, "So, is your practice here in Tallahassee?"

"Yes, it is. Still here after all these years. I worked in Orlando for a while, but there's no place like home. We all come home again one way or another," said JT.

"Yes, we do," said Nell. "I think it's time Ann and I went home, at least home to our husbands."

Ann looked at Nell as if she wanted to bite her, but she didn't resist when Nell tugged at her arm. She looked back at JT one last time. Her face broke his heart. He was still standing there, frozen in a crowded room when Judy walked over and took his arm. "Dance with me, cowboy," she said.

JT allowed Judy to walk him onto the dance floor and lead him around in some semblance of time to the music. Judy whispered to him, "Deep water, too deep to swim. You better come with me."

When the music stopped, JT allowed Judy to walk him back to their table as if he were a puppy on a leash. That's when he saw Sallie McGinty standing by the door searching the room. She soon saw her target walking toward her. She could spot a man with money like a bloodhound finds a bad guy. She grinned and said something to Beecher then the two of them walked out the door. She took her purse and jacket with her.

Ann sat quietly sipping her drink until she spotted another girlfriend on JT's side of the room. She hadn't seen her in more than ten years. She walked toward her friend as JT watched her. Her steps seemed somehow different, not quite so sure of herself as he remembered. He had heard rumors, so he wondered.

Beecher still had not come back into the room when Ann started to walk away from her friend. She turned around and found herself staring straight at JT's chest. She looked up, and he smiled at her. He held up his hand to take hers, and the two of them began to move to the music of time.

He whispered in her ear, "You are beautiful and smart, but most of all you are good and true. Never lose sight of who you are. You are the best life has to offer. Any man worth his salt could see that."

"You know, I think I've heard that line before. Some tall handsome blonde told me that twenty years ago. Do you remember that guy?" Ann asked with a soft smile.

Those words had echoed in Ann's ears for years. She wondered what had happened to the boy who spoke them. She wondered if he remembered or even if he had meant them, but most of all she wondered if she would see him at the reunion. That was the only reason she had agreed to attend. Now she had her answer, at least one of her answers.

"Yes, my dear, I remember him well. He made a grave error in judgment, and it has nearly destroyed him. Do you remember him?" JT asked.

"Unfortunately, I remember him every day. Sometimes I wish I didn't remember him so well, but I can't change that. Some things are written in stone, perhaps even before we know they exist. They are indelibly etched in our minds," Ann replied.

"Ann, I loved you the first time you spoke to me in the hall my senior year. I still feel the magic. That will never change," JT admitted.

"JT, I'm married. I can't change that. I have two children," said Ann.

"I know that. But I want you to know if you ever need me, I'll be there. Are you happy?" asked JT.

Ann laid her head on JT's chest for a short moment then looked up at him and replied, "I'm married."

JT had his answer. His heart hurt as he felt her body move with his. "I know, baby," he replied. The music stopped and he repeated, "I'll still be there if you ever need me." He took a small card with gold letters from his jacket pocket and gave it to her. It was a business card, but he had written his private number on the back of the card with the hope that he would have an opportunity to give it to her.

As she walked away from him holding the card, Beecher and Sallie walked back in the door. Beecher immediately saw the tall man with blonde hair walking away from his wife. By the time Ann got back to her table, Beecher was standing there glaring at her.

"Get your coat! We are leaving," he said. Nell saw his face and knew Ann was in trouble.

"Sit down, Beecher. We're having fun. Leave Ann alone," said Nell.

Buddy saw what had happened, so he patted Beecher on the back and said, "Sit down, Beech. Let's have another drink." Beecher had red lipstick smeared across his chin, a fact lost to no one.

Beecher sat down, but his expression didn't change. Five minutes later, Nell saw JT and Judy leave. She breathed a sigh of relief.

Beecher continued to drink one drink after another, getting drunker by the moment while Ann tried to laugh and chat with several friends who passed her table, but her heart was missing. She knew what lay ahead for her that night. She just didn't know how bad it would be.

The four of them got in Buddy's car just before midnight and drove away. Beecher had refused to spend the night at the hotel and was far too drunk to drive home.

When the car pulled up in front of the house on Smith Lake, Nell's gut was in a knot she would never forget. She feared for her friend and knew there was nothing she could do to protect her. Anything she said would anger Beecher even more. She had to hope he was too drunk to do much damage.

Ann got out of the car first and said goodnight to Nell and Buddy. Then she said, "Come on, Beecher. I'll help you inside."

Beecher shoved her away from him as he got out of the car. He slapped at the hand she held out to him. Nell jumped and gasped.

Buddy said, "It'll be ok, Nell. He's just drunk. He'll pass out before he gets to the bed." He wasn't far from right, but that was not enough to keep Ann safe.

Beecher stumbled into the living room and passed out on the sofa, but when he started to vomit, he fell to the floor. Ann tugged at him and tried to clean him up, but she was unable to lift him, so he lay face-down in his own vomit until the sun came up the next morning. Ann watched in horror as she feared he would aspirate some of the vomit and choke to death.

When he roused with the morning light, he shouted, "Ann, where the hell are you?"

Ann was in the kitchen making coffee to help him sober up, so she answered, "I'm right here, Beecher. I'm making you some coffee."

"Get in here, bitch!" Beecher shouted.

"I'm here, Beecher," said Ann as she stood over him with a cup of coffee.

Beecher looked up and kicked her, sending the hot coffee flying into her face. She was blinded for a moment, so as she ran from him, she ran into the rocking chair beside the fireplace and fell against the hearth. Beecher got up and loomed over her as she lay on the floor. He grabbed her arm and pulled her to her feet then he started to choke her. She could not scream because his wide thumbs had cut off her air supply, but even if she had screamed, there was no one to hear her screams.

When Beecher released her, she fell to the floor gasping for air. Beecher looked at her in disgust and kicked her in the ribs one last time. He went out the door and got in his truck. She heard him speed away, grazing two small black jack oaks as he fishtailed in the soft sand lane.

When she regained her strength, Ann got up and limped into her bathroom. She stood for an eternity in front of the mirror looking at her bloody face. She didn't recognize the woman she had become. How could she have become the helpless and battered woman she saw in the mirror?

8
HIDING ANN

Ann fled to her family's cabin at Indian Pass. She was too ashamed to face her parents and her friends. How would she explain the cuts and bruises? Why had she allowed herself to become a victim? She had no answers, only questions, the most pressing one: what was she going to do now?

The family kept a first aid kit in the kitchen under the sink, so that was her first thought. She set the kit on the kitchen counter and rummaged through it looking for antiseptic. She carefully cleaned the gash on her forehead where she had hit the hearth then filled an icepack to try to ease the bruises on her neck and body. Nothing helped. She opened the aspirin bottle and took out two tablets then stared at the bottle wondering how long it would take her to die if she took the whole bottle. Living through the day was not her top priority. She wasn't sure she wanted to see another sunrise.

She thought briefly about calling JT. She pulled the

card from her purse and looked at it. It represented a different life to her, one of safety, love, and security, but if she were to attempt to choose that life now, her choice would bring danger to JT, the one person she loved most. She could not do that. Her mind provided her with a vivid image of Beecher and JT. The image involved guns and blood, blood that would be forever on her hands. She would have nothing if she involved JT in her problems. She would lose it all.

Ann was Beecher's wife—he owned her lock, stock, and barrel. Both barrels were loaded, and he spent hours at the firing range. His arsenal grew each year, and he practiced regularly. He was a crack shot. One of his rifles had a long-range scope. He could kill JT without anyone even seeing him. He would kill JT if he ever suspected her true feelings for him. She had to find a way to let her dreams go and convince Beecher that JT was not a part of their lives.

It had been a grave mistake for her to dance with JT; she knew that even as she took his hand the night before. She knew what would happen, but she could not stop herself. She had to find a way to stop herself now to save JT. Her world was infinitely better when he was in it even if she was never able to touch him again, so she began to plan.

Nell was completely unaware of what had happened to Ann, but she became very fearful the next day when no one answered the phone at Ann's house. She didn't tell Buddy of her fears. She told Buddy she was going to Chipley to visit a cousin who had been sick. He believed her. She knew trouble was coming, so she didn't want

Buddy involved. She tucked a snub-nosed .38 into her bag and drove away in the direction of her cousin's house, but one block away, she turned the other direction and headed for Indian Pass. She had known Ann most of her life, so she knew where she would be.

Ann froze when she heard a car coming toward the cottage. She was terrified that Beecher would find her, but equally as frightened of her father's finding her. She knew what would happen if her father saw her condition. That result could be the same as if JT found her battered and bruised.

Ann held the curtains apart just enough to see the color of the car. She let the curtains fall back in place when she saw Nell's car, but she still trembled. What would she tell Nell? She had to find a way to let this pass. Any change in her life would bring harm to someone she loved. The only way she could protect them was to keep silent. Her wounds would heal. She didn't think Beecher would kill her, but if she told anyone what he had done to her, he would kill them. He loved her in his own way, so she believed he would never harm her seriously enough to put her in the hospital, but he would not hesitate to do so if someone came between him and her. He believed he owned her. He said God had given her to him; she was created for him as surely as Eve was created for Adam. She didn't much care anymore anyway.

Nell got out of her car cautiously. She looked around and saw only Ann's car outside the cottage. She hugged her bag to her side, making sure she could pull her gun with one motion. She walked slowly to the steps, watching for motion inside the cabin. Ann slowly opened the door before Nell reached the top step. She held the screen door wide for Nell to come in.

In a raspy voice, Ann said, "Come in." Her face was blank and dead with dried blood caked beneath one eye.

"Ann, what the hell happened to you?" Her hand went immediately to Ann's throat.

"I tripped and fell against the hearth," Ann said. She didn't realize until that moment that she could hardly speak.

"Fell, my ass! That bastard! I'll kill him! Where is he? I want him *now*!" shouted Nell. "Where are you, you rotten son of a bitch? Come out and face me like a man—oh, never mind—you aren't a man!" she continued.

"Nell, he isn't here. I came here alone. He won't come here. He knows better," Ann explained.

"Ann, he's crazy. You can't predict what he will do," said Nell. She took the revolver out of her bag and laid it on the table. "You don't have a gun, do you?" she asked.

"No, I don't and I don't want one. It won't come to that, Nell, because I won't let it. If I just keep quiet no one will get hurt," Ann said.

Nell plopped down on the sofa and said, "Oh, dear God! You really believe that don't you? Have you taken a look in the mirror? You are hurt, and I'm sure all the scars and bruises aren't even visible. They never are. I'm calling my cousin, Don. He's been on the police force for years. He knows how to handle men like Beecher. He will have a chat with your asshole husband, a chat he won't soon forget."

"No, no, please don't do that. If Beecher finds out I told anyone what he did, I'll be in a lot more trouble than I

am now. Please don't do that. I
know Don. I know what he thinks of men like Beecher, but you can't understand if you haven't been there. You can't stop them. Look at Beecher's dad. The only thing that stopped him from abusing Beecher's mom was her death. I'm sure she was relieved when she found out she had terminal cancer. I understand that feeling," Ann said. She had tears in her eyes, and the veins in her neck pulsed visibly against the dark purple finger marks across them.

"Ann, listen to yourself. You know Beecher is never going to stop this. Get out! We can protect you. We will. You must get out. Now!" said Nell.

"No, Nell, I can't. I have no money, no education, nothing. What would I do? Where would I go?" Ann asked.

"For starters, you come with me now," said Nell.

"I can't, Nell. You know that," replied Ann.

"No, I don't know that because it isn't true," begged Nell.

"And what would Buddy do? Would he take in his best friend's wife and risk a fight with his buddy? And what would my kids think? They adore their father. They would never believe he did this to me. They would be so embarrassed if they had to tell their friends their parents were getting a divorce. My family is all I have. Don't ask me to give that up. My mother adores Beecher. She takes great pride in the fact that no one in her family has ever gotten a divorce. Do you want her to support me? It won't happen. She believes in that master/slave relationship the Bible preaches. She says if you make your bed, you must lie in it. I've made my bed. Now I have to sleep in it for the rest of my life," said Ann.

"Ann, that is bullshit, and you know it! You know your family would take care of you," said Nell.

"They would for a while. Then what? What happens when they retire? Mother's health is not good. What happens when they are gone. I'm Mrs. Beckham. That's it. That's all there is to me. I lost Ann a long time ago. She left with the man in the green sedan. She's gone!" said Ann.

"Oh, not again!" said Nell.

Ann finally laughed and began explaining. "It's the man in the green sedan again. I told you about him. He's my boyfriend. Don't you remember? That's why I don't work in his office anymore. Now Beecher's going to target JT instead of the man in the green sedan if I can't convince him otherwise."

"He really is nuts, isn't he?" asked Nell.

"You tell me. He certainly sees things I don't see, but maybe I'm the crazy one. That's what Beecher says. He thinks I'm lying to him when I don't see what he sees. He took me out to the end of the driveway to show me the car then when it was not there, he said the man had left because he saw Beecher come home. He thinks the man won't show up when he's here. He sees the man's headlights at night sometimes. He even saw a boat on the lake one night at midnight then when I came outside, suddenly it was not there. He says the man stole some of his tools from the garage," Ann explained.

"Why doesn't he call the police?" asked Nell.

"Good question," replied Ann. "But most important of all, now I have to protect JT. Beecher is dangerous. No one knows that better than I do."

"JT is a big boy. He can take care of himself," said

Nell.

"You've never seen Beecher's arsenal, have you Nell?" asked Ann.

"No, should I?" asked Nell.

"No one is allowed in there except Buddy, but I know he brings home guns pretty often. I'm sure he's got more firepower than the local Sheriff. JT is no match for him. He is crazy, and he is sneaky. I couldn't live with myself if JT were to die because of me," said Ann. She hung her head and began to cry again.

"Oh, Ann, how did you get yourself in this mess? What can I do?" asked Nell.

"Nothing, just leave me be. I'll heal, and I'll go back for more. I have no choice," explained Ann.

"Ann, please leave. I understand what you are saying, but I can't stand by and let this happen to you," Nell begged.

"You don't have any choice either. Do you want to be the reason I die?" asked Ann.

Suddenly sensing the reality of the situation, Nell replied, "No, I don't. I think this is a little like trying to rescue a puppy in traffic. If you grab for him, he might run and run straight into the path of a car. You are a puppy in traffic, Ann."

"Probably so, but you'll have to let me find my own path. You can't help. Now it would be better for you to go and let me be. I'm alright. I'll stay here until I'm a little stronger then I'll go back, not home, but back. I think this is the only home I have. My mother's cancer has spread. We just got that news last week, so I have to be able to help her. I will survive, Nell. Go away and leave me, or you will get caught in the net with me. Please, go," begged Ann.

"I will go, but you have to promise to call me the next time this happens, and believe me—it will happen again," said Nell as she stood in the doorway.

"I will," said Ann, but they both knew she wouldn't.

Not long after Nell drove away, Ann heard another car in the driveway. It was one she did not recognize. When it came closer, she saw that Beecher was driving a new baby-blue Cadillac. She trembled as he got out of the car, but she stood with her feet planted on the front porch of the little cabin, the cabin that was her domain.

Beecher got out holding the keys to the beautiful new car. He walked slowly toward the porch, but he stopped short of the steps. He laid the keys on the bottom step. He took great care in straightening the keys and turning the silver tag face up. Engraved in the silver bar were the words: "Ann's Cadillac."

"This is for you, Ann. I'm so sorry I hurt you. I love you so much I just couldn't bear the thought of you with another man. I was drunk. That wasn't me. You know I never want to hurt you. I've bought you this new car. I know it can't make up for what I did, but please forgive me. My life would be nothing without you. You deserve the best, so I've bought this new Cadillac to show you how much I love you," Beecher said.

Ann looked at him, but she didn't speak. She never knew what to say to him when he came crawling back after beating her. He had always brought gifts after one of these incidents but never one this large. She stood like a statue at the top of the steps for a long minute then walked back inside and closed the door. Beecher heard the lock snap in place. He smiled to himself and got in her old Ford and drove away, leaving the new Cadillac and the keys with her. She'd come back—she always did.

Ann didn't leave the cabin for a week, but she called her father to check on her mother. He asked why she was so hoarse, so she told him she had a cold. Chemo was scheduled to start the following week, so she had to come home. She got in the new car and drove home on Sunday afternoon. The smell of the new white leather nauseated her. Never again would she enjoy the smell of a new car. She was sure Beecher would lie to her parents and tell them she wasn't in church because she was sick. She was right. He did.

When Ann got home, she put on a turtle neck shirt to hide the remaining bruises on her throat then applied enough makeup to cover the marks on her face and went to see her mother.

Mrs. White had lost so much weight, her cancer was obvious. She was pale and thin. Ann had never thought of her mother as frail, but today she faced that fact. Her mother was dying. She had to hold her life together, whatever the cost.

The coming weeks were difficult for the entire family. In early August, Cora White was buried on a cloudy Saturday afternoon. She was laid to rest with mounds of white roses for a canopy. Ann rode away from the cemetery in the back seat of a black limousine followed by Beecher driving her new Cadillac. Ann sat beside her father holding his hand. He patted her hand and said, "Well, kiddo, it's just you and me now." And so it was.

After Christmas that year, Mr. White showed up at

Ann's door on a mild winter day. "Ann," he said, "I'd like you to take a ride with me. I have something to talk to you about."

"Sure, Daddy," she replied. "Where are we going?"

"We are going down to Indian Pass. We need to have a talk, and I want to show you something," he said.

Ann looked at him and saw the sadness he would wear for the rest of his years. Her mother had been his axis. He seemed lost now without her. Ann knew she was the only thing keeping him afloat. "Okay, Daddy. What is this about?"

"Life, baby. It is about life," he answered.

"That's a pretty broad topic, Daddy. Can you be a little more precise?" Ann asked.

"Ann, does Beecher hit you?" Mr. White asked.

"Daddy, don't worry about me. I'm fine," Ann said.

He had his answer. "Ann, you know you can always come home, don't you?" he asked.

"Daddy, I don't need to come home. I'm ok. I can take care of myself," Ann insisted.

"Can you?" her father asked.

"Yes, I can," she replied.

"Do you?" he asked.

"Daddy, where is this coming from?" Ann asked.

"Baby, I have made some arrangements for you that I need to show you down at the cabin. I'm putting the house in your name, but I want you to promise me you will *never* allow anyone else to have his name on that deed. Do you understand?" Mr. White asked.

"That is your sanctuary for the rest of your life. You go down there sometimes and spend several days at a time alone, don't you?"

"Yes, I do. I love being there. I can think better there. It is peaceful," Ann answered.

"Beecher doesn't go with you, does he?" Mr. White asked.

Ann looked out the window to avoid facing her father. The swampy terrain had become mysterious as they approached the pass. She took a deep breath and replied, "No, I like to be alone there. It is a sacred place. I don't like to share it. It is my altar, my shrine."

"Yes, I thought as much," Mr. White said.

"How did you know about my trips down there?" Ann asked.

"Bubba at the bait shop told me. We've been friends since we were kids. He sees a lot more than you might think. He called me a year or two ago to talk to me about it. If anyone ever bothers you at the cabin, all you have to do is call Bubba," Mr. White said.

"I know. He's always very kind to me. I go in his store sometimes to pick up a loaf of bread or some soft drinks. He's always very friendly," said Ann.

"The first time he called me, he said you had a bruise on your face. Is that something you need to tell me about?" asked Mr. White.

"No, I don't know what you are talking about," said Ann. She shifted around in her seat and re-adjusted her seat belt. Then she pulled down the visor and looked in the vanity mirror.

"Don't you? Ann, you are aware of Beecher's indiscretions, aren't you?" asked Mr. White.

"Daddy, that's between Beecher and me. I don't

want to talk about it," Ann answered.

"Alright, we won't talk about it, but we are going to make certain *plans*. That is why we are here," Mr. White said as he pulled into the driveway of the little sanctuary at Indian Pass.

Ann looked at him with an uncomfortable stare. They both got out of the car and walked up the steps to the porch. Ann followed her father obediently but uncomfortably into the living room. A small fire was burning in the old stone fireplace, so the room was quite cozy. Two old rocking chairs were placed in front of the warm fire.

"Sit down, Ann," Mr. White said.

"Who made the fire, Daddy? Is someone else here?" Ann asked. She looked around nervously.

"No. Relax. I asked Bubba to come down this morning and start a fire for me. Sit down with me," he replied.

"He has a key to the cabin?" Ann asked.

"Yes, he does. He looks after it for me. That's how he knows when you come down here by yourself. He stops by nearly every day to make sure no one is bothering our property. He'll never intrude on your privacy. He just makes sure all is well. I've told him to call me if he sees Beecher here. This is not his property, and it is my intention that it never be his property. I can't stop you after I'm gone, but I hope you will honor my request," said Mr. White.

"Daddy, I didn't know you disliked him so much," Ann said.

"Didn't you?" asked Mr. White.

"No, I really didn't. Did Mother dislike him?" asked Ann.

"Not so much. She never saw the things I saw, and I chose not to tell her," replied Mr. White.

"Why not?" Ann asked.

"I didn't think it would help, and I knew it would worry her. She was sick for so long. I didn't want her to leave this world worrying about you. I kept a lot of things from her for her own peace of mind," Mr. White replied.

"Oh, Daddy, I'm so sorry. I hide things from myself for the same reasons. The kids have no idea…" and she stopped herself.

"No idea about what, Ann?" asked Mr. White.

"About the mess I've made of my life. Everyone is better off if I keep my problems to myself. Just let me be," said Ann. She got up and walked to the back door and stood staring out at the bayou. The water sparkled with life and joy, but the cabin did not. Mr. White came to her.

"Ann, you are not better off. Tell me what is wrong. Let me help you," Mr. White pleaded.

"Daddy, I'm not ready to talk about it. I'll tell you when the time comes," said Ann.

"Ann, come in here with me," said Mr. White as he walked into one of the small bedrooms.

Ann followed obediently and watched as her father opened the closet door. He knelt down on a braided rug between the bed and the closet then reached in his pocket and pulled out a small pocket knife. He opened the largest blade and slid it under one of the pine planks in the floor of the closet then lifted that plank and the one beside it. Underneath was a sealed cavity that held a metal box. He pulled the box out and took a small key from his jacket pocket. He inserted the key in the lock holding the box shut then opened it. The box held stacks of one hundred dollar bills. On top of the cash was a sheet of paper folded in thirds and a silver key.

Mr. White stood up and put the box on the bed. "Ann, there is money here for you to live on for a while if you need it. There is more in a safe deposit box at the bank. Here's the key to that box. This paper is a deed to the cabin. I have deeded it to you, *you alone*. It has a life estate clause, so that it remains in my possession until my death, but at that time, it automatically becomes yours. You will not have to do anything, and it will not show up in my will. I will start liquidating my assets, and the money will be in that safe deposit box, which only you know about or have access to. You don't need anyone to take care of you, and no one should ever be allowed to hurt you—*ever*," he said. Then he took out a stainless steel revolver and laid it in the box beside the money. "Just in case," he added.

"Daddy, why are you doing this?" Ann asked.

"Security, my security. I'll sleep better if you promise you will use this any time you need it," he replied.

Ann started to cry, so her father enfolded her in his arms. "Promise me you will use this if you need to?" he asked.

"Yes," Ann replied between sobs. They never spoke of it again, but each knew the truth that day.

Ann's father passed away in his sleep several years later. He had never been the same after he lost the love of his life, so Ann could not be too sad at his passing. She believed he was with her mother, but most of all she was relieved that he no longer had to witness her struggles. Ann shared her feelings with no one after that.

Nell had taken her own advice and started taking classes at the local community college. Four years later she earned a degree in criminology. She and Buddy got a divorce after that. Nell disappeared from Ann's life, leaving her completely isolated. Beecher reinforced this at every opportunity. He now had Ann where he wanted her, alone and sequestered in her house on Smith Lake. Not even neighbors were close enough to sense the danger.

The final battle began over the deed to the cabin, but Ann would not relent this time. She had made her father a promise. She was punished for not doing so, but she never relinquished the deed. Beecher was stunned that Ann's father had left so little money in his estate. Ann smiled when he railed about the issue, but she never divulged her secret, and Beecher never found the key.

Beecher's secrets became less secretive. Their friends and neighbors knew of his dalliances, but Ann kept quiet until he brought her home a case of gonorrhea. After she was treated, she never again allowed him to sleep in her bed, but they remained married. It was easier that way—at least it was for a while.

Ann was sixty years old when the final curtain fell. The life she had lived for most of her life ended when he became so paranoid, she could no longer reason with him. The man in the green sedan had evolved into a fictional lover whom he believed was stalking him and lurking outside the gate, waiting for Beecher to leave each morning. He was convinced the man was going to kill him to get Ann and all his money. Ironically, the man he believed was trying to do this was his own brother-in-law.

Beecher claimed to have voice recordings of their conversations and copies of diaries Ann kept to record her trysts, none of which ever existed. The only diaries Ann ever kept were the ones that eventually made their way to Emily Prentice's desk, and none of them included illicit affairs as Beecher had claimed. As for the recordings—when Beecher was asked in the divorce proceedings to produce them, he claimed they had been stolen by one of Ann's many lovers.

Beecher's paranoia had become a full-blown psychiatric disaster by that time. Beecher was a paranoid schizophrenic, one with an arsenal of fully loaded weapons. Many of the weapons had been purchased surreptitiously, so they were not traceable. No government entities were aware of their existence. The law cannot seize weapons they are not aware of, and only Buddy, Ann, and Beecher knew of their existence. Beecher was safe. Ann was too afraid to report the arsenal; Buddy had been roped into believing Beecher's stories, so he would not disclose what he knew; and Beecher whole-heartedly believed he needed them to defend what was his—Ann.

This is the milieu Ann found herself in when the final assault began.

9 ESCAPE

"God damn it, Ann! Where is he? I know he's here, or did you sneak him out the back door when you saw me coming?" Beecher bellowed as he kicked in the front door.

Ann clutched the dishcloth in her hands and backed up against the kitchen sink. She knew what was coming. Beecher stomped through the living room and into the kitchen where she stood, white as the dishcloth she held.

"Beecher, there is no one here except me. I don't know who you are talking about. I've been here all day—alone," Ann said.

He slapped her first across the face. Her head slung to one side, but no tears came. They had long since dried up. She wasn't afraid anymore. Nothing mattered.

"Don't give me that shit, bitch! I have secret microphones all around the house. I've been listening to your conversations all day. You think I'm too stupid to figure this out, don't you? You are the dumb bitch, not me. I've got it all on tape. I'll get that bastard. You just wait and see if I don't. You're not going to screw around on me anymore!" Beecher shouted as he struck her jaw with his closed fist.

Ann screamed then fell to the floor. She tried to push him away, but he overpowered her. Her struggles stopped when he kicked her in the side. Beecher, suddenly frightened that he had killed her, backed away. She was lying on the floor, pale and barely breathing. When he realized she was still alive, he kicked her one last time then left.

It was deep in the night when he returned. He quietly turned the knob on his bedroom door and found it locked, so he smiled. He went into the guest room and went to sleep. He had won—she was still there, and he believed she always would be. He had taught her a lesson this time. Maybe now she would get rid of her boyfriends.

That was a Friday night, so Beecher didn't have to work the next day. Just after daylight, Ann tiptoed quietly out of the bedroom and back to the kitchen. She got an ice bag out of the freezer and held it against her jaw. She knew the cut on her lip probably needed stitches, but if she went to the hospital, there would be questions. She had applied a butterfly bandage after he left the night before. The bleeding had stopped, but the left side of her face was swollen and blue. She had bitten her tongue when the blow landed, so she was unable to eat. The worst of it was the pain in her side. She was still unable to breathe without pain. He had cracked two of her ribs. It would be days before she returned to normal.

She was sitting on the back steps when Beecher woke. He came to the back door and looked out at her. For a moment he felt the old tug toward her, but that didn't last.

He opened the door and asked, "What's for breakfast?"

Ann turned around and looked at him over her glasses, but she didn't speak.

"I asked what is for breakfast?" he repeated.

"What would you like, dear?" Ann asked with a bite in her voice.

"Same as usual, bacon and eggs," he replied.

Ann didn't say anything, but she got up and walked back inside. He stepped aside to let her pass through the door. She went to the stove and pulled out two skillets then cooked his breakfast without saying a word. When she had finished, she set his plate on the table and walked back out to the porch overlooking the lake.

As she sat down, she saw a couple paddling a canoe around the shoreline. They were laughing and talking. The woman dipped her hand into the water and splashed her husband then they both laughed again. The sky was clear and blue without a single cloud. No breeze was blowing, so the lake looked like a huge mirror with a green frame. Birds were singing, and a fat chameleon scampered across the steps chasing lunch. He flicked out his tongue and flashed his bright red throat in pursuit of his prey. A tiny copy of the green lizard followed in his tracks, learning the ways of his world.

When Beecher had finished his breakfast, he came outside and stood behind Ann looking at the serene lake. "Ann, I have to go to Miami next week. I want you packed and ready to leave at 10:00 Tuesday morning."

"Beecher, I don't want to go to Miami. You know I hate that city," Ann protested. She had difficulty speaking because of the gash in her tongue, but Beecher never noticed.

"Just be ready when I tell you to. You know I'm not going to leave you here to entertain your lovers. I'm not as big a fool as you think. Get your shit together. You are going with me. That's settled," he said.

Ann thought to herself, "Yes, it is settled," but she didn't reply. Instead, she began making plans. Her father had made sure she could follow through with those plans.

Ann knew that when she left this time, it had to be permanent. There would be no going back. Her parents were both in the cemetery, and her friends had long since forgotten about her. Even the best of friendships can only survive so many rejections. Nell was the last to go.

Nell hated Beecher. She finally figured out she was never going to be able to talk to Ann without Beecher listening. He hated Nell as much as she hated him. She was divorced, so she lost even the contact through Buddy. After Nell graduated and went to work, she became more independent than ever, so her marriage began to fall apart one paycheck at a time. She took a job in Tampa to get away from her connections and memories, so she left the lives of her childhood friends behind along with the memories.

Buddy and Beecher still worked together, and Beecher told him about the men Ann was sneaking around with. Buddy was so bitter about his divorce, he believed everything Beecher told him. He thought all women were lying cheats. It was easy to toss Ann into that category because he never saw her anymore. After she stopped working in their office, he assumed she was either out spending Beecher's money or riding around with the man in the green sedan just as Beecher said she was. The only difference now was that Beecher said it was a Mercedes Benz instead of a green sedan.

Beecher controlled every aspect of her life—every aspect except the out her father had left her. He left cash, and he left the cabin. Beecher didn't know about the cash, and he had failed to get his name on the deed to the cabin, but certainly not for a lack of trying.

Beecher had to go to Miami to discuss a contract with a developer he was building homes for, and he insisted Ann go with him even though he knew she hated South Florida. The congestion and crime in the city frightened her, but Beecher said she would go, so she agreed.

Their airline tickets were in Beecher's pocket, and they were getting ready to go when Ann clutched her stomach and doubled over. She had swallowed ipecac syrup minutes before. She began to vomit on the way to the car.

"I think it was the shrimp I ate for dinner last night. I'm sure I have food poisoning. I can't go, Beecher," Ann pleaded then she vomited again barely missing Beecher's shoe.

"Damn it, Ann! You fuck up everything I do. Get back in the house. I'll go by myself. That's what you wanted anyway, isn't it? I know why you want me gone, but you'll pay for this," Beecher swore.

Ann vomited for another hour, but she was safe from Beecher. She ran to the bedroom and jerked the suitcase from the closet. She threw clothes in as fast as she could then got in her car and drove away. Beecher would be gone for a week, so she took the few possessions she had to have and went straight to Dave Carson's office. She had sent Carson a letter the week before explaining her situation and her plan. She knew Beecher didn't know him, so she pinned her hopes on his willingness to help her.

When she walked into his office and asked to see him, she looked like walking death. Her face was white and drawn and the remnants of Beecher's last assault lingered on her jaw.

When the receptionist saw her, she guessed who this was. She got up quickly and came to Ann. "Ma'am, can I help you? You don't look well," the woman said.

"I hope you will help me. I'm Ann Beckham. I sent Mr. Carson a letter last week," Ann said.

"We've been expecting you. Are you being followed, and do you need police assistance now?" the woman quickly asked.

"I'm safe for now. Beecher is on a plane headed for Miami," Ann replied.

"Are you certain?" asked the woman as she ushered her toward the back office.

"As certain as I can be. I think he probably got on the plane. He was negotiating an important contract in Miami, so I think he would have gotten on the plane no matter what I did," said Ann.

The receptionist opened the door to a small office and announced, "Mr. Carson, this is Ann Beckham."

"Thank you, Mrs. Meeks. Hold my calls and get Winston over here right away," said the young man behind the desk.

He got up and came to Ann. He took her hand and asked her to sit down. "Do you need me to call the police now?" he asked.

"No, my husband has left on a plane for Miami, and he doesn't know I'm here. He will not be back for a week. Can I file for divorce and get him served before he gets back?" Ann asked.

"No, but we can start the process and get a restraining order. We can also get you a body guard of sorts. I've asked Mrs. Meeks to have Winston Brown come to the office. He will accompany you until we can get this situation under control," said Carson.

Ann noticed the photo of Carson with a beautiful young woman and two children, whom she assumed to be his family. She smiled faintly at what life was supposed to be.

Winston Brown turned out to be a very likeable fellow, so Ann felt comfortable when she left Carson's office under his escort. Brown had her drive her car to a private garage where the car was stored until he could be certain she was safe. He then drove Ann to Indian Pass where he and an associate provided 24-hour guard for her. Legal proceedings were initiated and Beecher was served before he boarded the plane for his return flight. He was informed that a restraining order had been filed and that he would be allowed no contact with his wife.

Beecher was at Miami International Airport when the restraining order was served. Two guards accompanied the deputy serving the order. Beecher was advised of the seriousness of this process, and although he was sorely tempted to show his true colors, he did not. He did, however, seethe all the way home and was ready for a fight when his plane landed in Tallahassee. It took him two hours to gather his baggage and drive to Indian Pass where he knew Ann would be.

Brown and his partner knew when he left Tallahassee, so they were both waiting at the entrance to the property when Beecher turned off the highway. Brown's truck was blocking the path. Beecher considered ramming the truck, but at the last minute, he thought better of it. He slammed on his brakes and slid in the soft white sand, narrowly missing a large oak tree. He got out of the truck and was met by two very large men with weapons. Neither man had a pistol drawn, but both had shoulder holsters holding large bore guns.

"Stop right there, Mr. Beckham. You are trespassing and are about to violate a restraining order filed against you. I advise you to get back in your truck and leave immediately," said Brown.

"Fuck you! Get out of my way. This is my property, and my wife is in there, isn't she?" said Beecher.

"We have no intention of letting you into this property, and the property belongs to Ann White Beckham, not to you," said Brown.

"She's my wife and what is hers, is mine!" Beecher said.

"No, sir, that's not correct," said Brown as he and his partner advanced slowly toward Beecher.

"You think you are tough with your fancy guns. You'll need them to keep me away from my wife. Bet you wouldn't be so brave without guns," said Beecher. He didn't move away as they advanced.

"Mr. Beckham, we don't need these weapons to take care of you. I suggest you get in your truck now," said

Brown. He took two more steps toward Beecher and was now standing within striking distance.

Beecher looked up at the much larger man and his partner then snatched open the truck door. He got in and spun the truck around to leave the property. As soon as he did, Brown made one call to the deputy waiting a mile down the road and five minutes later, Beecher had a hefty speeding ticket and was in the back seat of the deputy's car on his way to jail. He attempted to take his rage out on the deputy and was charged with assaulting an officer.

Brown smiled at his partner when Beecher drove away. "It feels good to stop an asshole like that, doesn't it?"

"Sure does," his partner replied.

"I'll never understand why nice women like Mrs. Beckham wind up with the bad guys, but they seem to do it every time. Dave says she's been married to him for more than 40 years," Brown commented.

"I can only imagine what he has put her through," said Brown's partner. "Did you see the bruises on her face?"

"Yes, they were hard to miss. The best we can do is to see that it ends today. I have to admit I'd like him to challenge me—just once. That's all it would take," said Brown. Brown stood six feet four inches tall and weighed 250 pounds without an ounce of fat. His shirts had to be custom made to fit his biceps, and if he hit Beecher once, the problem would be solved. He tapped his closed right fist in his open left hand and made a slapping noise. "Just once," he repeated.

Winston Brown's sister had been killed by her

husband when he was only twelve years old. He had loved his sister more than life, and he saw her battered face before the funeral home took her away. He vowed that day to avenge her death, and he did. There was no chance Beecher would ever get past him.

Beecher did not try to come back to the cabin for many months, but he set about making sure Ann would get nothing from him. He withdrew all assets from their joint accounts, but he had been successfully hiding his earnings for years, so many of his assets were already in off-shore banks about which Ann knew nothing. She knew he was transacting some of his deals under the table, but she had no way to prove that and no way to find the money.

Since Ann had never been paid a salary, she had no recorded income and no verifiable work experience. She was lost and alone, so she spent nearly all of her time at the cabin. During that time, she pulled out her old diaries and tried to reconstruct her life in some meaningful manner. She sat on the porch each day reading a life that seemed never to have happened. It was a surreal experience, but slowly she began to understand what had happened to her.

When the reality struck home, she knew what she had to do. She would find a way to share her story so that young women caught in the web of abuse could see they were not alone. She had kept her pain inside her heart all her adult life, but in sharing some of that, she believed she might find, if not happiness, at least peace and reconciliation with a life endured rather than lived.

Dave Carson fought for Ann as if she were his own mother, but her children were not so supportive. Their father told them about Ann's alleged affair with his brother-in-law and her dalliances with her cousin, whom he said gave her gonorrhea, which she transferred to him. They believed him. They believed their poor devoted father suffered from a venereal disease because their mother cheated on him with her cousin. They steadfastly refused to believed that he had choked her almost to death, broken her ribs, nearly broken her jaw, and left her badly bruised so many times she couldn't count them. They were not in court the day their father mysteriously lost the tapes of Ann's indiscretions or when he misplaced the diaries he said she had kept about her lovers. They pitied him when he could not identify the mystery man who stalked him and came to his home when he was away. He never gave them proof: he couldn't because the people and events never existed beyond his own twisted mind.

  The children and even Nell, who came back to her side, would never know the hell she had lived through for 40 years. Even she could not or would not remember all of those days. The human mind has its own defense mechanisms—it has to if women like Ann are to survive.

  Nell became more supportive and stood beside her that final day in court when the divorce was granted, but Nell would never fully appreciate what her friend had been through. Nell was retired by that time, so she offered to come and stay with Ann for a while after the divorce was final, but Ann did not want company. She wanted to be alone—alone and at peace.

  Winston Brown still came by and checked on her occasionally, and he gave her his private number. He assured her he would be at her side quickly if she ever needed him. He was brusque and sometimes a bit crude, but he was gentle with her and ultimately protective.

Winston shared his story with Ann one rainy day under an umbrella on the beach at Indian Pass, so the two of them had a bond that would last the rest of their lives. He had been married once for a short time, but like most nice guys, he married the wrong woman. Instead of an "Ann," he married a "Beecher." He got out before he had children, but it was different for him. He was a man. His identity lay in his job, his career. Ann's identity was "Mrs. Beecher Beckham."

It took Ann more than a year to locate her lost identity. It involved hours and hours of reading and understanding her diary, the record she had faithfully kept of her life as it unfolded.

When she finally believed she understood the life recorded in those pages, she lost the shame she had carried so long. She bought a *Writers' Market* list of literary agents and chose one located in Orlando to share her story with. She didn't know why she chose the name, but Emily Prentice seemed like a good place to start. The story took place in Florida, and Emily lived in Florida. Emily was a stranger, so it was easier to share the details with her. Maybe she would understand. Ann had never thought of herself as a writer, but she hoped the story would stand on its own. It was a life, not a novel that she handed to the postal clerk.

"Anything liquid or perishable in the package ma'am," asked the polite woman in the blue postal uniform.

Ann laughed and replied, "No, just books. Only life is perishable. These are just dead trees with words printed on them."

"That will be $5.40, ma'am," the clerk replied. She stamped the yellow envelope and off went Ann's past traveling to Orlando and beyond.

What happened next stunned no one more than Ann. When she answered the phone, one part of her was shocked, but something deep inside knew what would happen next. Her story would ring bells for women all over the world who were struggling against an enemy or sometimes even against friends in a world that didn't understand. Emily Prentice, indeed, understood what she saw. She saw a life. Ann's life changed forever when she saw Emily walking toward her on the beach at Indian Pass.

I am Emily Prentice. I had the privilege of watching as we found Ann. She is a lovely person and my friend for life. Ann worked with me for the next six months and what resulted was *Pink Shadows*, the story of a woman who lived in the shadow of an evil man for 47 years and survived.

What surprised me most about Ann was that Even as she acknowledged the reality of the problems she had faced, she still believed in the fairy tale. She believed in love and kindness, but she had finally realized, she would never be Cinderella, and there was no prince riding up on a white horse to rescue her.

Ann's story unfolded slowly to me as I walked with her on the beach at Indian Pass. She was a fearful kitten that day I walked up to her on the beach, but today she is a tigress, holding her own in the jungle of life. She made numerous trips to Orlando to consult with editors and her publisher. She was shocked to find how many women either had been affected by domestic abuse or had known someone who was. Time became her friend as surely as it had been her enemy in the past.

Winston Brown became her friend and mine, but later he became more than that to me. He represents all that is good in man, and he helps us to stay grounded and see that Beecher is the anomaly and not the norm. It would be far too easy for Ann and for me to see life as something dominated by Beecher and his kind, but it isn't. When spring arrives again, I will become Emily Brown. We have together witnessed the rise of our loving friend Ann White.

The day the book was released, Winston and I stood behind Ann as she spoke to reporters. Winston had a dual purpose that day and in many of the days leading up to that moment. He always wears a nicely tailored sport coat, which conceals a loaded revolver, and he is always alert. He, better than any of us, knows how much danger we were facing. He applauds Ann at every turn for her bravery. I don't think she will ever fully realize the danger she was in. She continues to believe in goodness over evil as she shares her story with the world.

The *New York Times* reporter who interviewed Ann the day the book was released knew about danger. She had been a victim of abuse just as Ann had. Her review never admitted to such, but she shared her story with us and assured us *Pink Shadows* would get the notice it so richly deserved, and it did. Ann traveled with me to book signings in ten major cities over the next several months, but it was the signing in Tallahassee, Florida, that changed her life forever. It was as it had been, should have been, and always would be.

10 FINDING ANN

Sending the diaries to Emily had been the first step in Ann's path to finding who she really was, but JT was still missing. She knew she had made the greatest mistake of her life when she pushed him away in the summer of 1975. She would regret that decision for the rest of her life. She was so young…and so blind. She could only see what was in front of her face and not what lay ahead. If she could go back and start over, what changes she would make, but now she was beyond any of that. At least she thought she was until September.

Tallahassee was only an hour away from Indian Pass, and Emily had scheduled a book signing at a small privately owned book store on North Monroe. Monroe Street Books had stocked an ample supply and Emily had sent them posters to advertise *Pink Shadows*. Ann trembled as she drove up the coast and turned north toward Tallahassee. She thought about JT as she drove. She knew he lived in Tallahassee, but she didn't know where—she was afraid of knowing. His practice was on the north side of town, so as she drove, she glanced about at every traffic light, hoping to see him walking down the sidewalk or driving the car pulling up beside her. Her head knew how slim the chances were of this happening, but her heart increased the odds every time her foot touched the brake.

Finally she saw the book store with her posters displayed on an easel sitting on the sidewalk. She eased into the parking lot beside the shop and parked. She closed her eyes and took a deep breath. She had tossed her life out for everyone to see, and she wasn't sure she would ever be comfortable with that. Emily would be there to hold her hand, but she and Winston wouldn't arrive for another hour. What would she tell women who read her story? She felt as if she were walking naked down Main Street in her home town.

She got out of the car, inhaled deeply, and let out the breath slowly. She had looked danger in the face many times over that past fifty years, but she was more afraid today than she had ever been. Sometimes she wondered if putting her innermost thoughts out for viewing like Monday's laundry might not have been in her best interest. Facing readers in other cities somehow didn't seem so frightening as it did today in her home town.

Emily had hired an off-duty police officer to stand guard in the bookshop. Beecher was still under a restraining order, but Ann knew full well that a piece of paper meant nothing to him. No one could guess what he might do. Fear nearly paralyzed her, yet she still looked down the sidewalks with the one happy thought that sustained her: JT was somewhere in her world today and not so far away as before.

Ann walked hesitantly to the door and put her hand on the handle. Slowly she opened the door. A little bell attached to the door jingled, and a tall gray-haired woman behind the counter looked up. She smiled broadly and said, "Oh my goodness! I am so happy to meet you."

The woman rushed around the counter and hurried over to Ann. Ann smiled and reached out to shake her hand, but the woman embraced her with a warm hug and moist eyes. "Ann, you have no idea what you have done for me and for many other women who have walked in your shoes. You've opened conversations that had been silenced for so long. You've given us comfort in each other. Now we can openly support each other, if not without fear, then at least without shame. I can't tell you how embarrassed I was to allow anyone to know how I had been treated," she said.

Ann's fear became compassion as she smiled at the slightly younger version of herself. She put her hand on the woman's shoulder and said, "Thank you for sharing that with me. That is the reason I allowed my story to be published. I finally realized I had nothing to hide. For so long I believed that my husband was a good man. I thought if I just tried hard enough, it would get better. I didn't want to embarrass him by telling anyone what he was doing to me. It took me forty years to see that I was not the problem—that nothing I did or didn't do would change him."

"I understand completely. All of us feel that way. I think you will get to meet more sisters today than you ever dreamed. My name is Sarah, and I am your number one fan," said Sarah. She sparkled with enthusiasm and hope, making Ann feel as if her struggle was worthwhile.

At 10:00 am the shop opened for business. The first two customers came in with the little tinkling bell above their heads. They rushed over to Ann and introduced themselves.

The first woman held out her copy of the book to Ann and said, "Ann, would you sign my copy of your book? I was so deeply touched by your story, and I want you to know how grateful I am for your courage in sharing your life with us. My cousin walked in your shoes, but she never told me until she read your story. She had kept to herself and hidden the abuse for years. When she read your book, she found the strength to leave her abusive husband. She is in therapy now and is finally living in safety."

The woman standing beside her spoke up. She said very quietly, "I, too, want to thank you, Ann. Your story is far too common. I am a police officer, so I see your story repeated nearly every day. I'm going to be staying with you today to ensure your safety. I'm acutely aware of how much danger you might be in by just appearing here today. Do you think Mr. Beckham might show up?"

Ann smiled at the woman and said, "No, I don't think he will, but then I've too often misjudged him. I'm happy you are here." Ann looked at the young woman and was surprised by her gentle face. She wore a white linen jacket and trim navy pants. Ann could see the slight bulge beneath her jacket. She knew what it was and was glad it was there. She didn't want anything bad to happen to Beecher, but neither did she want to allow him to endanger other innocent lives.

The woman answered, "You are right not to try to

guess what he might do. My name is Nancy, and I'll be near you at all times. I know what he looks like, and I'll be watching the door. If you see anything or think at any time that I need to move closer to you or if you feel any threat at all, don't hesitate to say so."

Ann began to relax. She took the book from the first woman and sat down to sign it. Sarah had placed a small table in the far corner of the room where Ann could sit to sign books. A stack of copies sat on the edge of the desk and pens had been laid neatly at the side. A pink eyelet table cloth was draped over the table, and a comfortable chair waited for her. Ann realized that Nancy had taken a chair between her and the door and had picked up a copy of *Pink Shadows* and started reading, but she held the book in such a manner that she could glance frequently at the doorway. The tiny brass bell stood between them and harm.

Ann looked into the face of the woman who had handed her the book to sign. The woman smiled at her with tenderness and said, "How did you ever get the courage to tell your story? My friend didn't even tell me what she was going through until she read your book."

"I felt I needed to tell my story as the final leg of my escape. I knew that as long as I hid the truth, he still controlled me. I vowed he would no longer control me. I didn't have a choice," replied Ann.

"Are you afraid of him still?" the woman asked.

"No, I'm not. That doesn't mean I think I'm not in danger. It just means I will stand up to him until he gets the message and leaves me alone. An abused woman can never be free until she vows to live free or die. I will live free," said Ann. She straightened her back and asked, "What is your name?" She held her pen to the page waiting to sign the book.

"My name is Julie, but I'd like you to put my friend's name there. Her name is Shelly. I want her to have a signed copy so that she never gives in and goes back to her husband. He's pretty persuasive. I'm going to buy another copy for myself," Julie said.

Ann laughed and said, "Yes, I know that feeling well. They are all persuasive, and you want to believe them more than you can imagine. Are you married, Julie."

"Yes, I am, but my husband is nothing like Shelly's husband, Bill. My husband is one of the good guys, not perfect, but a really good guy. When he found out what was happening to Shelly, he went looking for Bill. Fortunately the police found him before my husband did," said Julie.

Ann laughed and said, "Well, hold onto your good guy, and tell him to let the police handle Shelly's husband. They probably have more guns than he does."

"That's what I told him. I didn't want him to get hurt, but he was so angry when Shelly told us what he had been doing to her, he couldn't help himself," Julie replied.

Nancy looked up from her book and said, "Keep your good guy safe, Julie. We will take care of the rest of them." Nancy pulled her jacket back to expose a badge attached to her belt.

Julie smiled and said, "Thank you for being here. Keep this beautiful lady safe."

"That's the plan," said Nancy as she got up and walked to the door. She scanned the sidewalk and sat back down.

By that time another woman had come to the table,

so Julie thanked Ann and walked over to the cash register to pay for her second copy of *Pink Shadows*.

A steady trickle of customers came and went then just before noon, Emily and Winston arrived. Emily swept in like a hurricane, as usual, followed by Winston, who was happy to be her shadow. "I'm sorry we're late. Traffic was a bitch all the way from I75. Have you had many people come in?" she asked.

"Yes, more than I anticipated. I am touched by the response I'm getting but a little dismayed as well. Before we started sharing the story, I had no idea my scenario was so common," said Ann. The room had cleared, and no customers were in the store, so Ann and Emily had a chance to talk to Sarah, the shop owner.

Sarah walked over to them and shook her head, "Poor Ann still thinks all men are good, bless her heart."

Emily chuckled and said, "You'd think she would have learned by now."

Ann chimed in and said, "But there have been so many good men in my life, I can't believe Beecher is the norm. I'll never believe that." She put her arm around Winston and continued, "See, this is proof that good men still exist."

Sarah said, "I wouldn't say Beecher is the norm, but there certainly are too many of his kind—and far too few like Mr. Brown!"

Nancy joined the conversation. She said, "Ladies, you just wouldn't believe the things I've seen. But, like Ann, I still recognize the good guys. I'm married to one of them, and my father is one of them. I know how men are supposed to treat women, so when I see a man abuse a woman or a child, I have no problem taking them down. Sometimes I come away from an arrest with a few bumps and bruises, but I always feel good when I have made the world safe for an innocent victim. My job certainly has risks, but it has enormous rewards. The worst days are when children are involved. Ann, did your husband ever harm your children?"

"No, I think that would have sent me over the edge. I would have left if he had. He beat me when no one was around to see. My children don't even believe me. They still think their dad is a saint. They have more or less abandoned me. They think I am an evil woman who hurt their dad," said Ann. She looked down at the desk, but the tears in her eyes were evident to all.

"I'm sorry, Ann. Most of the time they will also hit the children, and you may think you would have left, but most women with children don't. They think they have to endure whatever the man dishes out to keep a roof over their heads. They think they can protect the kids from him, but they usually can't. They fool themselves into thinking that way," said Nancy.

Ann dabbed her eyes with a tissue. "People don't realize how complicated it is. They think you can just leave, but that's not always true."

"No it isn't. No woman wants to take her kids to a shelter, and many don't even realize there are shelters. At best a shelter is temporary. So many of these women don't have an education or any way to get a job. Men seem to know which women are vulnerable," said Nancy.

"Yes, I realize I'm one of the lucky ones. My father left me a home to live in and some money, money Beecher didn't know I had. The irony is that I would probably still be with him if I hadn't had those assets. As he became more paranoid, he convinced everyone that I was running around on him," Ann said.

As she finished her sentence, the small bell above the door tinkled. Startled by the interruption of their conversation, all three of the women turned at once to the door. A tall thin man gently opened the door and stepped inside. His blonde hair had turned nearly white and his blue eyes looked like sapphires against his tanned face. He saw Ann and stopped. He breathed deeply and said, "Hello, Ann."

Ann stood up and walked slowly toward him in an orchestrated dance of time, marching the clock back 42 years. He waited for her without moving a muscle. Ann didn't say anything, but everyone knew from her expression who this man was. When she got to him, she reached up and put her arms around his neck. The man slid his arms around her waist and held her close to him. He could feel her trembling. He whispered in her ear. "You are beautiful and smart, but most of all you are good and true. Never lose sight of who you are. You are the best life has to offer. Any man worth his salt could see that."

Ann smiled and looked deeply into his face. "I think I've heard that before," she said.

JT kissed her tenderly then said, "Yes, but I was afraid you might have forgotten. I have to show up every twenty or thirty years to remind you. I was afraid your memory had slipped."

Ann kissed him again, and everyone in the room began to applaud. She took his hand and led him toward

Winston and the women. "Ladies and gentleman, in case you haven't figured this out, this is JT Stanton," she said.

Nancy extended her hand and said, "Pleased to meet you, Dr. Stanton. Somehow I figured out who you were. You didn't fit the description of the other man I thought might show up today." She laughed and opened her coat to show her badge and gun.

JT laughed and stepped back. "Guess I'm lucky I'm tall and blond," he said.

"Indeed you are!" said Nancy.

Ann said, "Ladies, this is the best man I ever knew, the love of my life."

"And she is mine," said JT quietly. He held Ann's hand and still felt her trembling. He would continue holding her hand until the trembling stopped.

JT whispered in Ann's ear. "I read your book. We have a lot to talk about, but you will *never, never* be hurt again," he said. He squeezed her hand and kissed her forehead.

The little bell jingled again, and two women came in chatting and laughing quietly. Their chatter stopped when they saw Ann, and their smiles faded. They walked over to Ann as she stood next to JT.

"Ann, my friend and I came to thank you for telling your story. Pardon me for addressing you by your first name, but somehow I can't bring myself to speak your former husband's name," said the first woman.

Ann smiled and said, "It's perfectly alright with me. I am Ann, not Mrs. Beckham any more. I've always been Ann, but for a while I lost her. She's back now."

The other woman spoke up and said, "Ann, I'm the

reason my friend thanks you. I walked in your shoes for more than twenty years until I read your story. After I read your story, my husband only struck me once more. When he did, I called 911, and it was over."

The first woman laughed and said, "Fortunately she called me first and it was *really* over! I live two houses down from her, so I was there before the police arrived. I had a nice little talk with the bastard. I brought my friends, Smith and Wesson, to convince him to keep his hands off her. I told him he definitely wouldn't be having sex anymore if he ever touched her again. Lorena Bobbitt's shenanigans would look like child's play compared to what was about to happen to him. He understood what I meant. He knew what I would shoot first. He already knew I hated him, and he knew how I felt about abusers. Plain and simple: they should be killed, no questions asked. In my world, the first time a man hits a woman, he would be taken to the town square and shot, first in the crotch then in the head…maybe we'd wait a while to aim at the head. I'm thinking maybe only the last bullet would hit his head."

"Wow! You don't mince words, do you?" said Nancy. "It is much safer to let the law handle it. Sometimes, men like that can be much more dangerous than people realize."

"So can I," the woman said. Her eyes said she meant what she said.

Nancy laughed and stepped back away from the conversation. She couldn't admit she agreed with the woman, so she just smiled and kept watching the door.

JT only let go of Ann's hand when she sat down to sign copies of her book for the two women.

When the two women left, Nancy said, "You ladies stay safe, and don't hesitate to call for help if you need it."

The women smiled and thanked her then she heard one of them whisper, "Did you see how that man was holding her hand the whole time we were talking to her. I bet that was JT Stanton!"

Customers came and went for the rest of the day. Most were women, but a few men spoke to Ann and thanked her. They had seen this kind of abuse with sisters, mothers, and friends and knew how difficult it was to stop. One said his sister had been murdered by a former boyfriend and that his mother had never recovered from the loss. He said she died of a broken heart six months after she lost her only daughter. There was an aura of sadness in the little shop with the tinkling bell, but a small scent of hope lingered also. JT was that hope.

Winston stood silent while this conversation progressed, but he saw Ann look at him several times.

Ann kept looking at JT as she signed each book. It was as if they had never been apart. The years were erased by each smile they exchanged. She couldn't wait to be alone with him and talk to him, but she already knew what they would say and how it would feel to have him touch her. She had a long memory.

Winston found a comfortable chair between Ann and the front door. He had checked the back door twice to make certain it was locked and bolted. His chair was across from Nancy. He smiled a crooked smile at Nancy as she sat down. She nodded knowingly. Each looked down the sidewalk and out into the street then back at Ann. Both of them stood as bulwarks against a storm, a sudden tornado or a rogue lightning strike. They tried to remain invisible to all except Ann.

Nancy stood up abruptly and stopped in the middle of a sentence. She put her hand on the door and watched as a black Dodge truck went past. She noted the tag number and relaxed. She stepped back and nearly knocked Winston down. They both laughed and sat back down.

"Is that the truck I need to watch for?" Winston asked.

"No, but one just like that. Winston, don't take this on. That's my job," Nancy said.

"Nancy, apparently Ann didn't tell you, but I'm more or less her body guard. I'm licensed and armed. I'm the one he faced when he tried to get to Ann when the restraining order was served. He knows me. I don't think he will challenge me again. I appreciate what you are saying, and I will let you lead, but I'll be right there with you. He'll have to get past both of us to harm anyone else. I won't allow him to hurt her again," Winston replied.

"He is not likely to try anything today. That's not his style. If he does, however, he will not succeed," said Nancy.

"Oh, no. He won't succeed today or ever again," said Winston.

JT walked over to them and joined the conversation. "I overheard your conversation, and I want you both to know how grateful I am," he said.

"JT, do you have a conceal carry permit?" Nancy asked.

"Yes," said JT. His square jaw tightened.

"Are you armed?" Nancy asked. She raised her

eyebrow and looked at his jacket. She thought she detected a slight bulge under the trim-cut gray coat.

"Yes," answered JT.

"I understand, Dr. Stanton. I know you want to protect Ann, but the best way to do that is to let the law handle it," warned Nancy.

"I realize that, but where was the law all those years?" asked JT. His face was red with anger, and he glared at the passing cars as if they were the enemy.

"You do realize we can't stop problems we don't know about, don't you? Victims are abusers' best advocates. They often protect the very people who are hurting them. That is what Ann did. I'm not blaming her. They virtually all do it. There are a million reasons, but they all do it—at least for a while," said Nancy.

"That all sounds good on paper, but you know the truth, and so do I," said JT.

"Believe me, I am as angry as you are," said Nancy.

"I doubt that! You don't know Ann," said JT.

"No, I don't know her. But you've never held the hand of a victim waiting for an ambulance to arrive and watched her breathe her last breath while her murderer fled to Jamaica, have you?" asked Nancy.

JT didn't answer. He looked at her with a cold stare thinking that could have been Ann, and he wasn't there. He got up and walked out onto the sidewalk. He paced back and forth as Ann continued to sign books and chat with customers. Finally he came back inside and sat down. Nancy didn't say anything, but reached across and patted his knee. He smiled faintly with strained lips.

At 6:00 the shop closed for the day, and all of them

breathed a collective sigh of relief.

Sarah said, "Let me lock up and I'd like you to join me in thanking Ann with coffee and cookies. Please come into the back room where I have a little table set up. It's my small way of celebrating the bravery of this special woman and her publisher."

"Thank you, Sarah. That's very sweet of you," said Ann.

The tension in the room eased when the door was locked. They followed Sarah into the break room. She had little pink napkins and cookies iced with pink icing.

"May your days be pink and filled with joy from now on, and may your days in the shadows be gone forever. Congratulations to you, Ann and Emily, for a job well done. I very much appreciate your being here today and sharing your lives with me. Help yourselves to coffee and cookies and to lives well lived," said Sarah as she poured the first cups of coffee.

They all relaxed and enjoyed chatting with each other. Ann wanted JT to know Winston and Emily and what they had done for her, so she brought them together and told them how much she loved each of them. Emily and Winston promised to visit often at the little cabin at Indian Pass.

Ann could wait no longer. She whispered to JT, "Let's go. It is time for life to begin."

JT picked up Ann's jacket and said to the group, "Ladies and gentleman, I've been requested to accompany my princess back to life, so we'll be leaving now. Thank you all for bringing her home to me."

Ann stood as JT slipped the jacket over her arms

then she turned around and put her arms around his waist. He wrapped her tightly as if he could keep her safe forever.

"Ann, let me drive you home. I think that would be better than my following you. I can't rest if you drive home by yourself," said JT.

"JT, I'll be fine. I've been looking out for myself for a while now," Ann said.

"But you don't need to do that anymore. Today may be more dangerous than usual. I'm sure Beecher isn't happy about having your story spread all around town. I just can't let you go home alone. Why don't you come to my house and we'll go back to Indian Pass tomorrow," offered JT.

JT looked down at Ann's tiny frame and put his hands on her face. She flinched and shuddered. JT closed his eyes and bowed his head. "Oh, baby, I'm so, so sorry. You never have to be afraid again. I would never hurt you," he said.

Ann looked up at him and said, "I'm sorry. Old habits die hard."

JT's hands continued to hold her face as softly as a rose holds the morning dew.

"Will you come home with me? Please," JT pleaded.

Nancy watched and smiled. She nodded to him.

Ann looked at JT for a long while then said, "Yes."

Nancy said, "Let me walk you to your car. Dr. Stanton is right, you know. Beecher may rear his ugly head today. This was an insult to his manhood, whatever that is. Why don't you let Winston take your car and park it in a safe place Beecher won't know about, and you go with Dr.

Stanton—wherever you want to go?"

"She's right, Ann. Let me take your car. Call me later, and Emily and I will bring it to you down at Indian Pass when you go home. You go with Dr. Stanton," Winston said. Then he added, "Nancy, do you think I need to follow them?"

"No, I think they will be alright, but I'll make sure extra patrols check Dr. Stanton's house all night. We'll keep them safe," Nancy replied.

All agreed on the plan, so Ann walked out holding onto JT as if he might evaporate. Nancy looked down the street in both directions, but she couldn't see around the corner. She walked with them to the car and waited until their doors were locked and seat belts buckled. They both waved to her as JT's silver Mercedes pulled away from the curb.

As they drove away, Ann asked, "Are you sure you want to do this, JT?"

"Do what?" he replied.

"Risk your life," Ann said.

"What do you mean?" asked JT.

"If Beecher sees me with you, he'll kill you," Ann said as if she were reporting on the weather.

"And you think that scares me?" JT asked.

"It should," replied Ann.

"Does it scare you?" JT asked.

"Of course, it does!" said Ann.

"Well, it doesn't scare me. It would just give me the opportunity to do something that should have been done years ago!" JT said. He reached over and took her hand. "Don't worry, sweetheart, I got it covered," he said. They drove on toward the Ravines, but he kept glancing in the rearview mirror.

The driveway into JT's house was steep and twisting but beautiful. Ann looked around her and smiled. The house was not large as she had assumed it would be. It was mostly cedar and glass and nestled into its setting as if it had grown there as part of the landscape. It sat atop a small ridge. The sun was setting and kind shadows fell quietly across the glass panels. Behind the glass she saw a welcoming room with comfortable chairs and a heavy granite fireplace. A large gray cat sat on the window ledge watching a lizard stalking a tiny cricket.

The garage door slid up its track and JT drove inside. He immediately closed the door back before he turned the engine off. He said, "Wait until I come around to your door."

She nodded and watched him as he walked all around the car, looking for anything unusual. He came to her door and opened it then leaned down and extended his hand. She took his hand and stepped out. They walked up several steps to the door into the house. When Ann walked in, she was at the same time surprised and not surprised.

They were in the kitchen. All was as she would have expected, but she had never thought about how JT lived each day, how he buttered his toast, how he rinsed the coffee cup and set it in the sink or put it in the dishwasher. His was never an every day dream, but one lived in the abstract. She suddenly wondered what was behind the cabinet doors and whether he used Splenda or Trulia in his coffee. She wondered if she should scramble his eggs or fry them with bacon. She wondered if his towels were white or a soft blue. She wondered about everything she had never dared to think about before.

JT laid his keys on the small secretary desk just inside the door and reached above the desk to reset the security panel. A tiny light flashed on the panel then he turned to Ann and stood looking at her with a small but definable smile.

Ann looked at him and asked, "What, what is it?"

JT didn't move but smiled softly and said, "I've always wondered what you would look like standing in my kitchen."

"Me too," said Ann. JT walked over to her and put his arm around her.

"Come in here and let's sit down and try to relax. You must have been stressed today. But it is over now. The first day is done. Beecher didn't rear his ugly head. He probably knows at this point he's lost his power," said JT.

"Don't ever be too sure about him. He's full of surprises," Ann said.

"So am I," said JT as he took off his jacket and laid it across the chair.

Ann laughed as she saw what he meant. He had a Ruger .357 revolver tucked into a shoulder holster. He took it out and laid it carefully on the end table beside the sofa.

"Ann, your daddy called me not long before he died. He handed me this revolver and asked me to make sure that if you ever needed me, I would take care of business. I promised him I would, and I will," JT said. His face was solemn but not sad.

Ann was taken aback. "My daddy told you that?"

"Yes, he knew more than you thought. He suspected

what was going on, but he was never sure. He said he had asked you if Beecher was hurting you, and you evaded his questions," JT explained.

"JT, I couldn't tell him. If I had, he would have killed Beecher then he would have gone to jail. I couldn't risk that. I thought it was better for my whole family for me to keep quiet. I thought I was protecting my father and my children. I tried very hard never to let them see what Beecher was doing, but it looks like that backfired on me," Ann explained.

"What do you mean, 'backfired' on you?" JT asked.

Ann sat down heavily on the leather sofa. She rubbed her hand across the smooth wood of the coffee table top and tried to explain. "JT, I always made excuses for Beecher to keep from hurting my children, so now they believe all the lies their father tells them. They think I was having affairs and cheating on their father. Believe me, never once did I even look at another man when I was married to their father."

JT sat down beside her and took her hand. "Ann if he had known you at all, he would have known you would not do that. That bastard! Do you think he is mentally ill?"

"Yes, I do. He even accused me of having an affair with my cousin in spite of the fact that he was always with me when my cousin came to visit. I think he actually believes his own lies. He accused me of getting gonorrhea from my cousin. Beecher gave it to me then accused me of giving it to him. He is totally nuts. He beat me for giving it to him when he was the one running around—not me. My doctor knew where it came from, but he just treated me and moved on to the next patient. I spent a week in hiding until the bruises healed after that encounter," Ann said.

JT got up and walked to the window. He stood staring into the deep ravine behind the house. Finally he pressed a button and the drapes on both sides of the living room closed. He walked back over to the table where he had put the revolver down and picked it up. He spun the cylinder then clicked it back in place. Ann watched him and knew what he was thinking.

"Don't, JT. Don't do it. He isn't worth it. I can't lose you again. I've suffered enough. Let the rest of the journey be the best part. Let it be only about us," said Ann.

"It will be, but you will always be safe from that crazy bastard. I promise you that! He will never hurt you again. I don't ever intend for you to be out of my sight again. I retired a couple of months ago when I found out that you were divorced. I don't intend for us to be apart for even an hour for the rest of our lives," said JT.

Ann smiled broadly and patted the seat beside her. "Then let's start the future now. Put the gun down and sit beside me. The future starts this moment. It is our time."

"But the future will not include Beecher Beckham. That is one thing I can assure you," said JT. "Any objection to changing your name, say maybe from Beckham to Stanton?"

"I'd say that would be a very positive change," said Ann.

So began the long conversation they had both waited a lifetime for. They walked out to the patio overlooking the ravine and sat down facing a wall of green. The air smelled of new life and wisteria growing on a tall pine. After the sun set, a silver moon rose above the trees and night sounds called to them. They sipped white wine and the nectar of honeysuckle vines.

Sometimes they talked and other times they were quiet so that life could penetrate their souls. Finally when JT saw Ann's eyes begin to struggle to stay open, he said, "Come inside, Ann. Come to bed with me. Let's have life as it was supposed to be before we got in the way."

Ann folded her hands in front of her mouth as if to pray and whispered, "Yes, let's."

Ann lay down beside JT and snuggled into his arms. She felt safe for the first time in almost half a century, but she wasn't, not yet.

Ann slept more peacefully than she had since the day she married Beecher. When JT woke, he slipped out of bed quietly and made coffee for Ann then returned to the bedroom and sat watching her sleep until her eyes opened. She jumped when she realized where she was then she saw him. She lay back down and took a deep breath. She smiled.

"Good morning, sunshine!" said JT.

"It is a good morning!" answered Ann.

"Yes, it is," said JT as he came to her side. "It is day two of the best part of our lives."

"JT, let's spend the day at Indian Pass and pretend the past didn't exist," said Ann.

"I like that idea. I think your daddy is probably waiting to see us there. That is where I met him when we had our final conversation," JT said.

"I guessed as much. That's where he always went when he had thinking to do. That was his refuge. He said his head was always clear when he got to Indian Pass. I'm sure he's waiting for us, but what if someone else is waiting for us there?" asked Ann.

"Well then, he'll have to go, won't he? That cabin is only big enough for two, and I'm not leaving," said JT.

JT walked over to his security system and checked the cameras then picked up his keys. "Let's go home," he said.

Ann's smile swept the lines from her face, and she followed him to the car. Ann called Winston and found out where her car was then they went downtown and Ann got into her car. JT waited for her to back out then pulled in behind her. He followed her car, never losing sight of her. The .357 was tucked into his shoulder holster once again.

The drive was quiet and peaceful. It was Sunday morning and the only traffic was the few families going to early church meetings, so Ann and JT were relaxed and hopeful at last. Both of them watched for the black Dodge truck, but none crossed their path. They reached the twisting drive into the cabin just before 9:00am. The morning sun was still cool in the trees and the water was calm when they walked out onto the back porch of the cabin.

The wind was sleepy but tiptoed quietly through the trees and brought the last remains of a fog that had hung over the bay earlier. The leaves were heavy with moisture and life. Small birds hopped about from branch to branch looking for acorns and insects. A large black and yellow bumblebee hovered near the eaves, threatening to bore into the old wooden structure.

Ann and JT sat holding hands and allowing the morning to unfold, relaxed and peaceful for the first time in many years. Ann said, "I know it's early, but don't you think we should have a glass of wine? Somehow it seems right."

"Sounds good to me, but anything sounds good to me right now," JT replied. "Tell me where the glasses are, and I'll get it."

"No, I'll get it. I'll be right back. You sit here and hold my place," Ann said. She got up and walked back inside.

JT watched the bay as two large mullet jumped and splashed back into the water. After a few minutes, he called out, "Can I help you in there?"

No one answered. "Ann, are you alright?" he asked. Still no answer then he heard a crash in the house.

JT jumped up from his chair and jerked the gun from its holster. "Ann," he screamed.

He was in the kitchen doorway in a second. What he saw turned his veins to ice. Beecher was holding Ann with a knife to her throat.

"Get out of here, JT. This is my wife. You won't get away with fucking my wife. I know you've been fucking her all these years, but you won't get another chance. Leave right now or I'll slit her throat, and you can watch her die. You might kill me, but you'll see her die first. Go! Or I'll kill her. If you want her to live, get out of here and leave her alone. She's *my wife!*" said Beecher.

JT stopped in his tracks. He held the revolver at his side but behind a lamp where he knew Beecher couldn't see it. "Beecher, you don't want her. Let her go. I'll leave, but you'll have to let her go if you want me to leave."

Ann quivered and her eyes were wide. She said,

"Beecher, honey, I didn't know you still loved me. Have you come back to me? You know I'll always love you. JT, you go back home. Beecher and I have to talk. He loves me and wants me to come back to him. You know that's what I really wanted all the time. You go back to Tallahassee."

Beecher grinned and said, "See, I told you she's my wife. Take your pansy ass on back to town, city boy. She wants a real man."

Beecher relaxed his grip on her and Ann said, "See, JT, Beecher loves me. You go back to town now."

Beecher laughed and moved the knife away from Ann's throat. When he did, Ann hit the floor. JT fired before Beecher could react. Beecher dropped to the floor beside Ann. Blood spurted across the room as his heart pumped one last time. Hot blood shot across Ann and soaked her face.

JT knelt beside her with blood running like a river across the floor. "Are you ok?" he asked.

"I don't know. I've never been so frightened in my life," Ann said. She clung to JT as he lifted her from the floor. They both looked down at Beecher. He was not breathing. He looked small and suddenly old as the color left his ruddy skin and seeped out onto the ever-reddening tile on the floor. Smells of life now became the stench of pain and death.

JT led Ann to the chairs on the porch and held her hand as she sat down like a robot being directed by a remote control. Then he took his phone from his pocket and dialed 911. "This is Dr. JT Stanton. We need assistance at Indian Pass. We are at the end of Oyster Shell Lane near the end of Indian Pass Road. There has been a shooting. A man is dead."

It seemed like an eternity before they heard the sirens. Officers swooped in with guns drawn, but they soon saw the danger was lying dead in a pool of blood. They were already alert to the threat Beecher posed.
Investigation determined that Beecher had hidden his truck in the trees and had been waiting in the closet for Ann to return. He had crept up behind her when she came into the kitchen.

When everyone finally left late that night, Ann turned to JT and said, "JT, do you know what would have happened if you hadn't been here?"

JT replied, "Why do you think your father gave me this gun and asked me to come?"

"When did he ask you to come?" asked Ann.

"The day before yesterday," replied JT in a kind whisper.

"You know he's been dead for two years, don't you?" said Ann.

"You really think so?" asked JT with a wry grin.

"I thought so. Maybe I need to talk to him now," replied Ann.

Ann walked back out onto the porch and looked back at JT. "I'll be back in a little while," she said.

A full moon lit the little path down to the bayou, and JT watched as Ann walked toward the water. When she got to the edge of the water, she sat down on a driftwood log. A large silver mullet jumped clear of the water and left rings of light all around him when he splashed back into his home. JT watched Ann blow a kiss to the moon fish as she got up. She walked briskly back up the path to the cabin and the love of her life.

"Daddy's happy now. He says it is as it always should have been," said Ann.

JT tucked her under his arm and walked her back to life.

"I decided it is better to scream. Silence is the real crime against humanity."

Nadezhda Mandelstam

OTHER BOOKS BY THIS AUTHOR

Behind the Tupelo Tree

A Civil War

The Ghost of Blackwater Creek

Illusions of Honor

Eminent Danger

B'ar Yarns

Blue Butterfly Days

Holocaust in the Homeland

The Magic Dolphin

Salem's Theocracy

Thomas Wolfe: Aline Bernstein's Dark Brooding Flower

Shooter Giggers

Made in the USA
Columbia, SC
20 July 2017